'In the kingdom of the blind, the one-eyed man is kinky'

—*Selected Declarations of Dependence*, Harry Mathews

Contents

THE UNIVERSITY OF BLISS

CHAPTER ONE

G LADYS WIPED the steam off the bathroom mirror and saw herself emerging from behind a cloud. Terry's installation of the ventilation system hadn't worked.

'We can't have the Vice-Chancellor losing herself in a great fog.'

Foolish man. Now she could see herself properly she liked what she could see. An attractive woman in her late forties who had scraped herself out of a grubby northern town and had found in its place a large bouquet of flowers. Just make sure you don't drop them, she said to herself.

There were bottles of Coco Chanel, several foot lotions and a bottle of Le Brexit in the bathroom, that spectacular French perfume which cost an arm and two legs and was hard to get hold of now that trade between the UK and Europe was a source of endless aggravation. Le Brexit, for all its loveliness, seemed to say: Dear English friends—stick to black puddings and if you're feeling unloved drown yourselves in a cauldron of tea.

The bathroom smelt gorgeous. Gladys could hear her husband bumbling around. 'Would you like some coffee from that new Neapolitan machine?' he called out.

She puckered her mouth and embarked on those lip stretching exercises she'd read about in *Women Avanti!*—an online magazine aimed at female captains of industry or as they put it, Sisters of Success. My body is my temple is my Caribbean account . . .

She would have liked to have been a little taller but she was agile and had never abandoned her passion for karate. She'd been good at sports and there'd been no hesitation in making her captain of the girls' hockey team at the Academy of Unhindered Progress in that faraway city Shudderfield-on-Sea.

Terry called her the cat. Sometimes he called her lolly pop. He had his uses and almost always gave her his undivided attention when it came to matters of importance.

Of all the parts of her body she loved most it was her feet that did it. When Terry lifted one of them to his lips, muttering 'Pure bliss', she felt a surge of blood to the pelvic area.

'Stop that!' she said, pretending to push him away.

'I know what my Gladys likes,' he said, as if he were a lusty game keeper rather than a middle-aged man with a paunch.

The best way he could make her come, they discovered long ago, was kissing each foot and making strange noises at the same time or better still—their favourite Sunday afternoon activity—sucking her toes having clicked onto Blotify so as to listen to an endless looping version of Anita Baker's 'You Bring Me Joy'.

This was the moment the first name of the Vice-Chancellor-in-waiting collided with her rather unusual surname: Gladys Nirvana.

Terry had never been very impressive in the groin department but the way he handled her feet was sublime. If she'd had more time she wouldn't have minded coming right now. There was, however, a scheduled meeting with the Reverend Lady Bishop in the Senior Common Room and she didn't want to be late.

There was a lingering residue of propriety in her professional dealings with members of Senior Management including the Bishop whom she'd met at a charity function.

Terry laid down the foot. 'I'll get the car ready,' he said.

Things had gone well for so long. She'd stepped inside a virtuous circle and once there she had no intention of stepping out. She had won a scholarship to a good university. She worked hard. Her postgrad studies in entomology allowed her to go on that notorious field trip to Colombia where she claimed to have discovered a new species of ant.

Filching some information from one of her professors, she published her paper on The Nascent Hexapod. Gladys liked to think of them working selflessly for their queen. Although she finished her doctorate in record time she realised there wasn't any money in the world of insects unless she sold out to the Pentagon where they were cloning a giant species which would be used to police the Mexican border. She met an American general in Tampa, a friend of the President, yet he seemed so crazed Gladys had to get out of the room in a hurry.

Being an obscure, if respected, entomologist sweating in a South American jungle or spending hours in some anodyne laboratory seemed rather limiting.

Her friends said, 'Have you considered running a university? There's an awful lot of money in it for Vice-Chancellors.'

Student fees continued to rise after the pandemics of 2020 and 2025 and the outbreak of Gorilla Pox in 2030. Most academics were on zero-hour contracts. Several made use of food banks, one of the country's growth areas. They might trade their PhD for a bag of groceries.

If you ignored the rising rate of suicides among the staff the bureaucrats' take-over of the universities had been a bloodless revolution.

Erasmus groaned in his Swiss grave so frequently his exhalations had given birth to The Tree of Misery, which some wit had dubbed The Toblerone Crucifix.

Chapter Two

'Thirty-eight, divorced, mother of two sons, a woman is masturbating in her bedroom with a thick, supple dildo. She has resorted to the instrument after weeks of general chastity and is now using it to achieve her sixth consecutive orgasm.'

—*The Way Home*, Harry Mathews

He Office of Continuous Improvement was run by Roxana Grogan whose intellectual triumphs included a brace of Wow Techs. Not having any academic qualifications didn't deter her from striding across the campus with purpose. She was supported by a team of middle-class women with swinging lanyards. Their improvements were constant and deleterious, successfully sabotaging the smallest flicker of scholarly activity.

The Department of Wellbeing organised compulsory wellbeing sessions. Demoralised staff were obliged to stroke a dog which sat impassively in the middle of an unhappy circle. Even the dog was depressed.

At the end of the year academics were expected to take part in the Play and Creativity Festival. A large marquee was erected outside the library. Points were given to staff who played the part of a Fool, Shakespearian or otherwise. Fools' Hats were sold in the Campus Shop. They were expensive but the cost could be deducted from the lecturer's salary. The purchase of a hat was more or less compulsory. Professor Leech, the Dean of Discipline, sent timely reminders.

The university had installed a rigorous surveillance system. Doomails were checked assiduously. Any behaviour deemed non-compliant was investigated at speed. The Dean spent his days firing off diktats.

The University of Bliss had a Branding and Marketing Centre run by Saffron Fraud OBE. Branding exercises were cascaded across the university and marketing consultants were paid lots of money.

Saffron organised weekly team meetings. 'Give me some old codswallop and I'll brand it for you,' she liked to say.

'Don't you have to believe in the brand?' one of her younger colleagues asked.

'Course not—you have to get other people to believe in it. Remember, surfaces have depths. Whatever his faults Goebbels knew his stuff when it came to branding.'

'Why not call it the University of Codswallop?'

'Not such a bad idea.'

Teaching staff with good ideas were given a twenty pound 'hat voucher' and a letter of thanks from the Vice-Chancellor.

Simple slogans illuminated the university: Be Good Enough, Reach for the Possible, Read Only When You Feel The Urge, The University Is All About You, This Is The Place to Explode.

Fred Clueless, Head Librarian, had a photograph of Philip Larkin in some kind of derriere-garde gesture. He had decided books were taking up too much space. To discourage scholarship, staff were charged to take books out and fined heftily for books that were returned late. Most of the books had disappeared anyway and the lecturers would sometimes sing quietly to themselves: 'Where have all the flowers gone? Long Time Passing. Where has all the learning gone?'

There was a graveyard next to the campus where the corpses, inspired by the work of Stanley Spencer, ventured into the light, looked in horror at the world around them, and clambered back into the ground.

Clueless said, 'Money might be better spent by bringing in Learning Love Pods where students can sit in circles interconnected by their g-phones listening to a high energy remix of "The Revolution Will Not Be Televised." '

The idea of television seemed so retro several students had a panic attack and when, in a moment of derring-do, Clueless showed a clip of an old-fashioned library in which there were tables and books and people reading in absolute silence some of the students were so upset they had to book in for Instant Aggravated Wellbeing Sessions.

Mr Clueless was threatened with disciplinary procedures. He showed the Dean how much money he'd saved cancelling journal subscriptions and he was let off with a slapped wrist.

The University of Bliss had an inclusive LGBTQIAYK[-INK -]Z± programme and transitioning in both directions—either on a permanent or temporary basis—was smiled upon. Gender fluidity obfuscated the government's scrutiny of gender pay and Senior Management noted the effort put into changing gender distracted staff from their inevitable descent into intellectual bondage. The Campus Shop sold an array of accoutrements and expensive lingerie. The university boasted it had more deluxe gender-neutral lavatories than any other university in the country.

There was a team dedicated to the writing of Mission Statements. They had a background in advertising. Not one of them knew

George Orwell had written 'Advertising is the rattling of a stick inside a swill bucket.'

A good Mission Statement could earn a tidy bonus and there was no stinting of effort. There were a few recycled favourites like We Believe In Nice Things or It's Nice to be Nice Even Nicer to be Even Nicer or Freedom of Speech is OK But Watch What You Say! Remember Hedgehogs Have Feelings Too or, When it Rains The Grass Gets Wet, Don't Forget Your Kagool!

Professor Leech kept a beady eye on these *obiter dicta* and sometimes got on his Super X Wob Top and threw in a few of his own: Inanity is the New Sanity, he snarled in a moment of satisfaction.

Or DON'T JOIN THE CALIPHATE RE-CALIBRATE!

The team were spurred on by the Dean's linguistic prowess and they strove harder. Anodyne Is The New Paradigm and Mental Health Is A Source of Wealth were much praised and earned a Team Bonus Plus Award on the Intranet Motion Lotion Media Road Test APP.

Roxana Grogan from the Office of Continuous Improvement sent a suggestion of her own. Anything she wrote had to be checked but on this occasion it came out as WE ARE A SPONGE CAKE—YOU ARE THE JAM IN THE MIDDLE.

'That's cool,' said Nikki, trainee Mission Statement Writer.

The Mission Statement Team worked with Saffron Fraud of the Branding Centre to create a Wob Wob Page. Senior Management were so pleased they threw a prosecco and pizza party in the Fairly Old Building. The Wob showed happy students silhouetted in dappled light. It was evidently filmed in the summer and young men and women ran through the long grass until they got to the ocean which was Mediterranean blue. Here the happy youths undressed to reveal perfect bodies and leapt into the water.

Part of the video showed a student looking at a medieval manuscript. Counselling was offered immediately but days later the young man was found hanging in the Forest. The *Chronicle* was instructed not to report the incident and the student's name was quietly erased from the University Attendance Register.

Everything on the Wob was perfect and even Professor Leech allowed himself a half smile. Other than the medieval manuscript there was little evidence any learning occurred at the University of Bliss. One of the history lecturers had been asked to wear an academic gown and there was a cameo moment in which he was shown playfully dodging Frisbees on a manicured lawn.

The film didn't show the Frisbee hitting him in the back of the neck.

The Reverend Lady Bishop—Imelda Wellbeloved—ambled around the campus with a Shih Tzu. The dog had been flown over from the factory in Tibet at great expense. There was a range of Shih Tzus available but Imelda had gone for the luxury model. A top of the range Shih Tzu could glow in the dark—as could its excrement—which the dog generously spread around the campus far and wide in small, illuminated packages.

The Student Volunteer Scheme encouraged students to become Shih Tzu poop scoopers—something for the CV—and they were incentivized by a Zapp which allowed them to use a high-tech Poop-Nav Ping-Pong Bat which had the magnetic force to suck the excrement from a considerable distance and at great speed. Having shot through the air the luminous crap hit the ping pong bat with a satisfying smack.

The experience was heightened if a member of staff inadvertently stepped into the flight path.

The Bishop had a pooper scooper of her own but she could never find it, buried as it was beneath a pile of Gnostic Texts. Eric

Smallbone, her Buddhist colleague -Acting Head of the Theology Department—found it difficult to disguise his mirth.

The Shih Tzu was called Ethelred. Imelda had him neutered which aligned with the university's non-binary policies. He would never be ready for procreation but the removal of his testicles seemed to have activated his anal glands thus Ethelred the unready became Ethelred the shitter—the university mascot—whose name could be conveniently shortened to Ethel.

Ethelred's testicles were buried in a pot and the unexpected growth of a Shih Tzu tree convinced the Pro-Vice-Chancellor she had been anointed by higher powers.

Imelda looked out of the window. It was snowing lightly and the campus looked beautiful. If the temperature dropped any more she'd get out those ear-gloves especially knitted for her Tibetan dog. They had a purple hue and matched her robe as well as her short hair which she liked to dye variously, often in the colours of a rainbow, but today was a purple day.

Imelda was happy and worried. Happy her niece had gone to the trouble of knitting the ear gloves but worried that the theological pulse at the university was throbbing less strongly than it should. It was her job as Pro-Vice-Chancellor and Proctor of the Church of the Aubergine to keep marketization in line with doctrinal beliefs. She wanted to be sure the new Vice-Chancellor was skilled enough in the art of duplicity to allow revenue streams to enrich the university without compromising spiritual values.

Who didn't want to work for a well-endowed university?

The Church of the Aubergine had broken away from the Church of England. There were strong emotional connections and no real theological conflict though the new church had set up its own hierarchy and was now sourced financially by an American evangelist called The Light of Idaho.

It was difficult to know the gender of the Divine Person but Imelda rebuked herself for such diluvian thinking. The Light of Idaho had installed an ecclesiastical hot phone in the Bishop's office and even now Imelda wondered whether the Divinity Line would break the silence with a Gregorian chant. A call from Idaho! It was so nice to hear that soft American voice and any worries she had were soothed away.

Imelda found herself composing a new mission statement, a gentle reminder to the less theologically equipped members of Senior Management. 'Jesus was a carpenter,' she wrote, 'think what he would have achieved had he graduated from the University of Bliss!'

The Church of the Aubergine had found inspiration in Julian of Norwich. The church enjoyed a combination of vagueness and ritual. Its belief system was not based on the scriptures as such—though the *Song of Songs* was sometimes evoked—but rather on a series of charismatic accidents. The discovery of the Weeping Eggplant/Aubergine had created a contemporary narrative which the church authorities grafted on with joy.

Aubergines were prized for their colour and shape and the weeping vegetable became as lucrative as a holy relic in the Middle Ages. A new range of shoe wear had been designed. The Berlusconi-Gucci line was somewhat niche. Imelda got several pairs of boots on university expenses.

The University of Bliss held onto some notion of faith which was not unconnected with the fifteenth century theologian Denis the Carthusian. That was a long time ago. By 2035 the Church of the Aubergine was alive and kicking.

The Light of Idaho had hinted to Wellbeloved the lachrymose eggplant could be given on loan to the university and the thought of it sent Imelda into a transcendental funk. She could barely stop herself from rolling in the snow. Only the thought of Ethelred's promiscuous anal glands tempered her enthusiasm.

Representations of the aubergine—sometimes in weeping mode and sometimes sanguine and serene—were found across the campus. The university had entered into discreet negotiations with Jeff Koons. He drew up a model of a giant eggplant rising up from the graveyard.

There was a commanding sculpture on top of the New Building called Redemption: Our Lady Of Aubergines. Some mornings Imelda woke in state of ecstasy having dreamt she had become Julian of Micheldever.

Imelda put the Shih Tzu on the lead and made her way to the campus chapel where she attached a notice. Friday next: the Eucharist followed by a ploughman's lunch. All welcome. Students and staff of all faiths and students and staff of no faith.

The University of Bliss had slipped fifty places down the League Table. This is why the governors had insisted on getting Gladys Nirvana. She knew how to shake things up and furthermore she'd written a book.

Pure Reflectivity was a best seller. Senior Management couldn't stop themselves looking at the bibliography to see if their article on Time Management had been cited. Imelda Wellbeloved was pleased Nirvana had made a reference to her own—brilliant—critique of aubergine eschatology. She would have liked a more extravagantly generous appraisal but it was reassuring to see that Nirvana could cut through one layer of bullshit to find a completely new one.

Nirvana had realised from the beginning of her academic career that reflectivity was an apparatus of control. Instead of writing a book about Greek philosophy the academic would spend their time reflecting on why they wanted to write it which meant the book never got written. The perfect result. Who wanted books anyway? Not the Head Librarian.

A scientist by training, Gladys had a contempt for the humanities and the university did not as yet have an Entomology Department. That was something she wanted to bring up with the Bishop. They did have a Maggot Racing Stall at the Play and Creative Festival which was popular with students who named the maggots after those academics who'd refused to award them a first-class degree.

What had Orwell said about the future? Imagine a boot stamping on a human face—forever. A handful of melancholic lecturers at the University of Bliss felt the future had arrived. Like Elizabethan courtiers they sent hand-written sonnets to each other, escaping Professor Leech's surveillance system.

Before switching off the light at night, Tristan Black—Senior Lecturer and melancholic poet—looked longingly at the portrait of Antonio Gramsci hanging by the door.

In 2035 there were Reflective Facilitators, Wellbeing Tutors, Knowledge Replenishers, Staff Study Buddies and Please-Stop-Me-and-Ask-A-Dumb-Question Visiting Lecturers.

Professor Leech liked the fact that after the Head of English had been found hanging in his office he was the only professor on campus, apart from the Vice-Chancellor of course, the Bishop and that woman in charge of Play and Creativity. And Humph Lacan—who was a fucking disgrace.

Senior Management had insisted on uniforms, cost deducted from salaries. The union dragged itself out of retirement and organised an old-fashioned Sit In. The managers alongside the administrators were disturbed by the sight of those drab academics holding drab books. They felt a tinge of pity and for the time being made the wearing of uniforms voluntary. Younger members of staff could be seen wearing their Team Bliss T-shirts in the summer.

In the 1970s *The Joy of Sex* was a best seller.

In 2035 there were various editions of *The Joy of Bureaucracy*. No lack of franchising and spin-offs either. The University of Bliss patented a reality game called Master Bureaucrat. An opportunity for likeminded people across the sector to display bureaucratic skills in a time pressured reality show. It involved databases and a woman's silky voice saying 'Matt has prepared a killer spreadsheet full of numbers going up and down the page. He's taken the frozen excrement of an Arctic rabbit and melted it in a jus of fiscal rectitude and drizzled the sauce over the spreadsheet creating a dish of intense tedium with a hint of smugness.'

The University sent a Quality and Development Manager to Rome. The Italians had enjoyed two thousand years of Byzantine chicanery and were happy to trade bureaucratic secrets for large sums of money.

Much eating took place in the Eternal City. Convenient to have a University Gold Plus Expenses Card in the inside pocket of one's recently acquired Italian jacket. The Bliss Team met with the Vice-Chancellor of La Sapienza University—'Il Magnifico Rettore'—known by his students as the Magnificent Rectum.

A line of bespoke bureaucratic socks was designed. Blessed by the Pope and splashed with Holy Water they were available in an understated English grey and were hard wearing if somewhat itchy.

A new line in lavatory paper too, a brand called Excel-In-Lent. 'The perfect way of pampering one's bureaucratic bottom after a long day sitting on it!'

When Gladys had checked the proofs of her book she turned to Terry and said, 'This is going to put my name on the map.'

'What's that my dear?' He was nodding off on the couch.

'I said this reflectivity shit's got legs. I'm going to make us a lot of money honey.'

'I should jolly well coco Yoko,' Terry said and began to snore.

He can massage my feet later, Gladys thought to herself and threw him an angry glance. She made her way to the kitchen to crack open another bottle of Sauvignon. The price of French wines had quadrupled in the last two years. She fired off a message to an old friend in Shudderfield-on-Sea. She thought about a line of coke. She did her favourite karate move instead.

Pure Reflectivity was Nirvana's Little Red Book. The revolution needed to purge the academy of useless old fools who argued education was a public good. *Pure Reflectivity* was the bible of the university police, neo-Calvinist capitalists clutching Toblerone Crucifixes.

Reflect, pull down thy vanity, practice permeability, practice humility! Let your mind rot. Reflect a bit more! There was always some dog to stroke.

Nirvana appeared on *Point of View*, a late-night programme on the BBC. These days Mary Beard was sporting a beard of her own. Gladys deflected Beard's questions, which were too complicated for the author of *Pure Reflectivity*. At one moment Gladys crossed her legs to reveal a pair of Berlusconi-Gucci boots. Terry poured himself a glass of Old Poultney. That's Gladys for you! Little minx. She's becoming a public intellectual. It won't be long before she gets a gong—an OBE perhaps!

Terry addressed his wife directly: 'I've bought a pot of foot lotion—peppermint, basil and cucumber—hurry home, lolly pop!'

Roxana Grogan was on the interview panel to make up the numbers. She'd been tasked with asking this question: 'Gladys, what has been the greatest moment of your career thus far?' That day, awed by the presence of the author of *Pure Reflectivity*, she couldn't speak. Her lanyard hung quietly for once and her glasses steamed up.

The interview was a big money interview. Nirvana would accept the position of Vice-Chancellor if they offered a 'substantial package'. The salary would be accompanied by private medical insurance and first-class travel on planes and trains and a generous expenses allowance. She wouldn't need a chauffeur as her semi-retired husband could take on that role.

'So you see,' she argued, 'I'll be saving you money!'

Imelda listened. She found it distasteful that Nirvana was bereft of subtlety. At one point it looked as if Nirvana might decline the offer. She was writing down figures on a piece of paper. '£900,000 seems—all in all—a little on the stingy side. This is 2035! To be frank I would be expecting at least a million and what's more I'd say that's a rather conservative figure.'

The stand-off was eased by Professor Leech who leant forward with a hint of halitosis. 'I'm sure we can find a mutually acceptable way of moving this forward.'

Gladys smiled. She realised that the Dean, notwithstanding his reputation, might be someone who could do her bidding. She offered him a peppermint.

'That's settled then,' Nirvana said. 'There's one steep League Table to climb, time to get our ladders out ladies and gentlemen!' And then she added 'Not to mention my colleagues who are neither one nor the other.'

Derek Nobody squeezed his Kegel muscles. He'd been in charge of Human Resources so long no one remembered how he'd got the job.

The Pro-Vice-Chancellor gave a tenth of her salary to the church and believed members of Senior Management ought to do the same.

She said: 'Render to Caesar the things that are Caesar's . . .'

Gladys had read about the Church and its money-pumping HQ in Idaho. The thought of it made her vagina itch and she wanted to start scratching. The first time she'd come to the campus she'd seen the great aubergine on top of the New Building—Redemption: Our Lady Of Aubergines—and she was seized by a visceral clutch. Redemption! So primitive. Yet follow the money, she reminded herself, pay lip service to the Light of Idaho. Stretch those lips, swing those hips, Sister of Success . . .

Nirvana would play the long game. Smile sweetly at the plump Bishop. One day she would turn her into a cockroach and put her in a laboratory in that yet to be created Department of Entomology.

'Imelda,' she said, 'every academic institution should subscribe to a set of core values.' She pushed her arm across the table and touched the Bishop's finger: 'Oh Bishop Wellbeloved, I feel it in my heart. All shall be swell, all manner of things shall be swell.'

That'll show the sanctimonious bitch, she thought to herself.

The following day Nirvana received a call asking if she would like to accept the job.

CHAPTER THREE

ERRY, AN ACCOUNTANT, went through the contract and passed it over to a friend who was a lawyer.

'It looks dandy to me; just need to keep that churchy stuff under control. The Bishop is some kind of *éminence grise*. Make as much money as you can but don't take your eye off the ball lolly pop. You know what I think? I think we should buy an enormous property close to the university.'

'Could do,' Gladys said, and went off to run a bath. She shouted from the landing 'I'm going to have a soak and dangle my feet over the edge.'

'What's that, darling?'

Gladys chucked a soap bomb in the bath.

Terry brought the Jag to a smooth stop and Gladys got out at the main reception. It was a few days before Easter and the snow had finally gone leaving the campus beatified with magnolia trees and the scent of fennel. A student volunteer in a Team Bliss track suit welcomed the newly appointed Vice-Chancellor and walked with her to the Senior Common Room. Gladys couldn't help thinking there ought to be a little more fanfare but this was an unofficial visit as she wasn't in post until September. Imelda Wellbeloved, Pro-Vice-Chancellor, was standing in a purple gown, Ethelred was sitting at her feet and the dog was wearing purple ear-warmers in case the weather turned again.

The Bishop walked towards the Vice-Chancellor and kissed her cheeks. Gladys got a whiff of cannabis oil.

'Vice-Chancellor—oh Gladys—welcome to the University of Bliss!'

A special tea had been prepared, a pyramid of cakes and sandwiches. Catering had gone into VIP mode.

Imelda turned to the student, 'You may go now.' And then she said to Nirvana: 'You are not officially in position yet but I thought we could chat about a couple of things before the hurly burly.'

'You look stunning Imelda!'

The Shih Tzu growled and the Bishop said, 'Stop that!' She gave the dog a kick. 'Ignore Ethelred. It takes him a while to get used to strangers.'

Gladys bent down and gave the Shih Tzu a piece of cake. The dog licked it and dropped it on the floor. When the Vice-Chancellor-in-waiting looked up she noticed half a dozen aubergines skating across a frozen lake in a mauve painting.

'How was the journey down?'

'My husband drove. They have their uses,' she joked.

Imelda had never felt the need for one herself.

Imelda continued, 'Unprecedented times, Gladys, as you know. Important we present a united front.' The Bishop had taken on the role of tea-pourer, and the Earl Grey was poured into a china cup, decorated with purple initials UOB, which some students pronounced Yob. Welcome to the University of Yob.

'I can't wait to get stuck in,' said the Vice-Chancellor. If Nirvana had been alone she would have pulled off a karate move.

'We need to keep an eye on the finances. Thankfully, Professor Leech is particularly good at that.'

As long as he doesn't rein in the Vice-Chancellor's expenses, Gladys thought to herself.

'Maximum student satisfaction too, I would hope,' offered the Vice-Chancellor.

'Our aim is a perpetual 100-percent Gold Satisfaction Rating,' Imelda replied, 'If one of the Learning Replenishers doesn't meet their target we haul them over the coals more quickly than they can say PhD. Staff Study Buddies are given opportunities to improve their customer service skills and work closely with student focus groups. We seek to neutralise any independent thinking. We prefer to fill the minds of our staff with pictures of small animals, something nice.'

'Quite right. I think we can agree on that.' Though why bother with something nice, Gladys thought.

'That one's vegan,' said the Bishop, pointing at a mauve-coloured cup cake.

She continued, 'We're piloting a 115 percent Super Plus Satisfaction Model, but we have to work round the maths on that.'

'Any issues regarding gender-neutral toilets?' enquired Gladys. She didn't give a toss but felt it was a safe question to ask.

'I told you at interview our gender-neutral lavatories are the best in the country.' A hint of excitement in the Bishop's voice. 'For three years running we won the Gold Shine University Lavatory Award. One year we whisked the title away from the University of Bath, from under their very noses!'

A bit of carrot cake had got wedged into the Vice-Chancellor's upper palate and Gladys used her tongue to dislodge it. The dog looked at her and Gladys could have sworn its tail lit up.

The conversation bumped along pleasantly. No need to stray into controversy at this stage and of course their managerial standing would be strengthened if they made sure the university climbed the League Table. Two big egos in the Senior Common Room. Imelda wanted to make sure Gladys understood the importance of the Aubergine. It was her trump card. She had spoken with The Light of Idaho and she had a bespoke ecclesiastical phone installed in her office! The university prided itself on its spiritual values and the Vice-Chancellor, hardnosed materialist though she was, would have to accept that. The Bishop argued that spirituality could be enshrined within the market place.

Gladys brought up the subject of work protocols. 'I'm presuming we have a clear system of demarcation?'

'Yes,' the Bishop said. 'Only highly paid members of staff can live in Trollop Town. Lecturers have to live in agreed designated places and commute in by train. You need a very high citizen score to own a car.'

'Good, presumably they return home immediately they've completed their day's work?'

'Of course. We are following the government's line on financial classification and appropriate employee spacing ratios.'

'That's a relief. I always thought the apartheid system had things going for it'.

'There were winners and losers.'

'I like to bat for the winning side myself.'

The Bishop sipped her tea. 'I want to share something with you.'

Gladys tilted her head and unbeknownst to her Ethelred tilted his head too.

'This is off the record so I would prefer it to stay *entre nous*.'

'I beg your pardon,' said Gladys. Languages had never been her strong point.

'Mum's the word,' the Bishop said, raising her finger to her meaty lips.

The Vice-Chancellor attempted a smile.

'The thing is,' said Imelda, as if about to slip into a trance, and lowering her voice a little, 'the Light of Idaho has intimated that he, or rather they, might lend us the Weeping Aubergine for an indefinite period.'

'The original?' asked Gladys.

'There's only one Weeping Aubergine,' the Bishop said. She went on: 'The University of Bliss would become a place of pilgrimages, the new Canterbury. We would become the gatekeepers. As you might imagine,' she continued, 'the university would be in an excellent position to make a lot of money and we would also be able to organise international theological conferences and a series of interactive symposia. A good moment to introduce a postgrad course on Resurrection Studies too.'

Let's concentrate on the dosh, thought Gladys.

'You remember that old expression "blended learning"?' asked Imelda. 'We could create a blended paradise.'

What a load of old crap, thought Gladys, but she feigned interest.

'As Vice-Chancellor your position would be greatly enhanced. We'd have the revenue and the prestige to challenge the leading universities. Our spiritual brand would be highly marketable. Good for the League Table and good for impact scores too.'

Somewhere in Gladys's head she could hear that old song by The Pet Shop Boys: 'I've Got the Brains, You've Got the Looks, Let's Make Lots of Money.' Mind you she had the brains and the looks, and the feet. She was thinking of a villa in Italy, a bespoke team of reflexologists. She could have her own handpicked live in personal trainer. Terry could go for long walks. It would be good for him.

The women sipped their tea. They heard the thud of a tennis ball followed by a loud expletive. Sunlight poured into the room. Imelda felt blessed.

'The Church of the Aubergine is ecumenical,' she said. 'If you'd prefer to call the aubergine an eggplant that would be perfectly acceptable.'

Gladys looked at the skating aubergines and wondered how much you could charge a Chinese student to touch the Weeping Vegetable or just get near to it. Ethelred rolled on its back, its little penis pointing upwards. The Bishop bent down and stroked his tummy.

'Tell me,' asked the Vice-Chancellor, 'are the staff docile?'

'We've done a good number on them over the years and your book is required reading. I prefer to use the term "self-effacing".'

'Docile and self-effacing seem an ideal combination,' Gladys said. 'I'm big on compliance. I'd like a maximum employee compliance ratio.'

'You'll certainly have Professor Leech, the Dean of Discipline, on your side and the union has been more or less emasculated,' said the Bishop.

Ethelred whimpered.

'I need everyone singing from the same hymn sheet.' Gladys enjoyed throwing in a religious metaphor.

'We do like a singsong in the chapel,' the Bishop said. 'Actually you might be interested to know I've written a few hymns myself.'

'Any recalcitrant staff?' asked Gladys.

'A few older members of staff still have a quaint belief in the value of education.'

'Why haven't you sacked them?'

'They've been with us a long time. They're on the old contracts, Gladys, and they serve a purpose on Open Days. You can't go around sacking everyone.'

'I made a good job of it when I was at the University of Great Expectations.'

'We like to think we manage our staff, how can I put it, in a spiritually enabling way,' the Bishop said.

'They should be spiritually enabled to leave. Are there any staff members I should know about?' Gladys asked.

'We do have our triumvirate of troublemakers, as I like to call them.'

'A triumvirate! That's rather a lot, isn't it?

'Humph Lacan is French, or at least French when he wants to be,' said Imelda. 'He's distantly related to Jacques Lacan.'

'Who?'

'You know, that French intellectual, the mirror stage, etc.'

I'm happy to drink French wine, thought Gladys, but I don't want the university besmirched by European intellectuals.

'He's a bit of a linguistic terrorist, our Humph,' continued the Bishop. 'It obviously runs in the family.'

Gladys felt herself getting hot. Bad enough having to think about aubergines.

'He has a thing about the signifier—he likes switching signs around. Professor Leech got quite worked up. He found Roxana Grogan trying on some experimental underwear in the ladies' lavatory, which had been until very recently the men's lavatory if you catch my drift. I shouldn't really have told you but anyway he was so embarrassed he wanted to have Humph sacked, or rather *Onfroy*'—she pronounced his name with a French accent—'but Lacan had won the International Leonora Carrington Prize at the Edinburgh Festival. He'd switched so many signs around the capital was in meltdown. The police arrested him but he said chaos was the point. It was a performance! The judges thought it cutting edge and he was interviewed by the BBC on that special arts programme, the one hardly anyone watches. Senior Management offered him a chair before they understood the implications.'

'I see,' said Gladys, appalled.

'All work no play makes Jack a dull boy,' said the Bishop.

Gladys said, 'Nothing wrong with old fashioned dullness.'

Imelda poured some more tea. 'There's a couple more you should keep your eye on.'

'Tell me,' Gladys said, getting out her notebook.

'Tristan Black and Harry Blink, both poets. They teach Creative Writing.'

'Creative Writing!' she spluttered, 'don't you mean Creative Shite-ing!'

The Bishop who didn't approve of bad language laughed and laughed. They laughed like old girls at a school reunion.

Chapter Four

A quasi-subversive organization founded recently in Prague encourages its members to invent obstacles to overcome while masturbating, The organisation is called Masturbation and Its Discontents. The first task set by the English chapter is to complete masturbation while reciting Milton's 'Il Penseroso'.

—*The Way Home*, Harry Mathews

HARRY BLINK blinked. It took him several seconds to realise it was morning. He could hear his Romanian neighbours humping. It was a high ceiling but it was a thin ceiling. There weren't any acoustic barriers in the building and it would have had to have been a state of the art acoustic barrier to muffle Norbert's grunting. On an average day he weighed in at eighteen stone, rather more after a week's consumption of Domino Pizzas.

The thought of Norbert slumped over Natasha wasn't good. She got her own back at weekends by delivering song-cycles of lamentation which made the wolves back home howl and the bears weep and the mushrooms roam across Europe like a new virus.

Natasha the Nag. She had every right to be. It was payback time. Norbert slumped on the sofa and sucked it up, his cock shrivelled like a scallop under waves of undulating flesh. Harry sometimes wondered whether Norbert pimped her out. He was always buying

La-La Cars which he parked outside their rotting Victorian building and which he washed and hoovered ostentatiously with the latest Zapp—Smash the Crap—Car App.

'Morning,' he said, gold chain around his neck, trackies billowing from ham-sized thighs. Harry thought about lending him *Mansfield Pork*, that lesser-known novel.

Harry didn't want to live in South Town. That grim conurbation. University teachers could rent a modest property there. They needed a middling citizen score to obtain their residence permit. A lower score meant North Town, or—God forbid—Shit Town. If his citizen score dipped he could be re-located at any moment. Disciplinary proceedings meant academics got sent to Shit Town for three-month tasters, on half pay and with limited access to toilet paper. In any case South Town was shitty enough.

Sometimes the train stopped at Shit Town. The air full of faecal odours. Travellers rushed to close the windows. An automated voice announced: 'This is Shit Town. Please don't alight unless you live here. Please don't alight unless you live here. This is Shit Town . . .'

Harry looked at the miserable bastards getting off. Wasn't that Terry Eagleton?

From South Town Harry took the Bliss Service to the university. He held his Bliss Movement Card which monitored departure and arrival times. Punctuality ratings were part of his annual appraisal. Harry had an annual thirty-minute credit allowance; if he went beyond that he was docked £10 per minute.

The train brought staff to the campus. The station was on the other side of the graveyard, next to Trollop Towers. Tickets weren't cheap.

'If you fail to produce a valid ticket you will be prosecuted. You could receive a custodial sentence,' the automatic train voice announced.

If you chose to stay home on a non-teaching day you had to write a working at home report. Compulsory to refer to Nirvana's *Pure Reflectivity*. It took most of the day to write the report.

Staff had protested against Professor Leech's plan to install an At Home App in all university software. The idea had been shelved but it was suspected he had found some way of spying nevertheless. When Harry wasn't using his University Wob Top he put it in the wardrobe. Sometimes he placed a small speaker alongside it and played a particularly frothy version of Serge Gainsborg and Jane Birkin singing *Je t'aime*. Then he had the terrible thought Leech might be jerking off in the panopticon office.

Je t'aime. Je t'aime. Oh pull away Leechy! Pull away!

It was easier to go to work and play with the Great Lego Set which had been handed out to every staff member at the International Lego Play and Creativity Conference.

Harry lobbed the pieces of Lego into his office bin. He described it—in his end of year Wellbeing Report—as a sedentary version of basketball and Penelope Peacock, the Professor of Play and Creativity, thought it an excellent use of his time and asked him whether he would like to be on a Do-Be-Do-University-Wow Tube.

'Give it some thought Dr Blink. We encourage creativity in all its manifestations and you've clearly got a considerable amount of talent.'

The early Bliss Train left South Town at six AM. There were scores of university staff with Chip and Go lanyards round their necks. Cost deducted from salary. Lost lanyards generating substantial fines.

Harry didn't like wearing his lanyard on the train, he didn't like wearing his lanyard anywhere. This generated nervous looks from younger colleagues. They preferred not to sit next to him. Different if it were Tristan Black or Humph Lacan. Now there was an outbreak of mirth and the sharing of scurrilous sonnets.

There was always a member of Senior Management or some lurking administrator ready to set him right 'Dr Blink, not wearing our lanyard today?'

He was tempted to say 'No, because I shoved it up the Dean's arse.' He smiled and said, 'It must be somewhere in my pocket,' and he made a show of looking for it and putting it around his neck.

'Much better Dr Blink.'

The Six AM Bliss Train was full of Facilitators, Knowledge Replenishers, Staff Study Buddies, Ask Me A Dumb Question Visiting Lecturers.

'Welcome to the Bliss Train, you are in one of four coaches. This is the service to the University of Bliss which stops at Brackenhurst. We hope you enjoy your journey. Have a great day!'

The train zipped through fields and past villages, sometimes cows and horses appeared then receded into the distance, or there was dog walker who stopped a moment to look. Staff slept or listened to their g-phones, some were dreaming of their g-spot. The journey took the best part of an hour. Some academics looked out of the window and contemplated self-immolation.

The automated American voice announced there was an at-seat trolley service—serving cookies, pretzels, coffees, teas, soft drinks including bottled water, and don't forget the Special Breakfast Bliss Deal which comes with your own pocket-sized edition of *Pure Reflectivity* and the Cod-Pod in which you can hear edited highlights spoken by Professor Nirvana herself. Use your Bliss Movement Card to make purchases. We aim to make your day a fabulous one!

The trolley man had once been a senior lecturer in European history. He lost his job when he published *The Year of '68*. Roxana Grogan saw an online review which used the French phrase Soixante-Huite, which she mistook for Soixante-Neuf, her only knowledge of the French language. She imagined it was a book about sexual positions with a salacious Gallic angle and she paid 'good money for it' only to find it was about uprisings of a different kind.

Not only did she feel she'd wasted her money she remembered the online Vigilant Training Course she set up at great expense and realised it was her duty to refer the matter of 'Soixante-Huite' to Senior Management. Dr Philips was almost encouraging 'Thinking' and it was agreed there should be an immediate disciplinary hearing. Ms Grogan punched the air.

Wasn't it enough to have reflected on the idea of writing the book rather than actually going ahead and writing the fucking thing? Wouldn't pure reflection have persuaded him against such an outlandish project? He argued it was a legitimate area of historical research but the committee of blank faces stared him down across the boardroom table. Imelda tried a kindlier approach—she was Church Proctor and Pro-Vice-Chancellor of a university which celebrated spiritual values.

She stood up in her Berlusconi-Gucci boots and smiled. A smallish aubergine fell out of her pocket and rolled across the room. The aubergine came to a halt and eyes switched back to the Bishop. 'If we were to be charitable Dr Philips, we could say you were guilty of old-fashioned thinking! This is 2035, no need to go scraping around in the 1960s, and in France too.'

The committee sneered.

Imelda shook her head. 'Dr Philips, I think we should re-name you Dr Inappropriate Philips. Guilty of wrongful, unnecessary, too clever by half thinking!'

Imelda was Bishop and grand inquisitor. 'I'd like to take a lenient approach but that depends on how willing you are to atone for this silly billy venture. I really don't want to say 1968 ever again, in any language. Do I make myself clear?'

Dr Inappropriate looked appropriately chastened.

'We could have you moved to Shit Town immediately. I could call the authorities right now. You'd be queuing round the block for cheap toilet paper before you could say Shih Tzu.'

Dr Philips could already smell the faecal matter.

'We could send you to a Pure Reflectivity Rehabilitation Centre.'

A PRRC. The post-Brexit equivalent of a North Korean gulag—unpaid labour and ten hours a day of vacuous propaganda. At the end of six months the only utterance which came out of the rehabilitated person's mouth was an inarticulate spasm: *Nirvana! Nirvana!*

'What have you got to say for yourself Dr Inappropriate?'

He bowed his head, 'I was seized by a scholarly urge.'

'Disgusting!' shouted Roxana Grogan, her lanyard bobbing up and down.

'Well now,' tempered Imelda, she felt Roxana could be a little unsophisticated at times, 'Dr Study Buddy Philips PhD, I think you should sit outside on that chair in the corridor whilst the Committee of Academic Correction and Real World Knowledge comes up with a considered response.'

Philips sat on a chair and wept. Stories of the PRRC were horrifying and he didn't like the idea of Shit Town either. He wondered if he should sneak into one of the gender-neutral lavatories and grab a couple of bog rolls.

Thirty minutes later the door of the board room opened and Roxana Grogan appeared. She jerked her thumb. 'You'd better get your ass in here ASAP.'

He went back in and sat down.

The Bishop smiled. 'Guess what? You can start cheering up! We've ruled out a PRRC and even Shit Town might be put to one side if you go along with our plan.'

Philips felt some relief. Though Shit Town would be unbearable you might push through to the other side, but no one survived a PRRC with their sanity intact. Post-PRRC subjects ended up in one of the new supermarkets acquired by the university stacking shelves for the rest of their lives and pissing themselves a great deal because pissing was about the only pleasure left to them.

'This is the document you have to sign. We will give you a few moments to think about it but if you don't sign it you can expect a much worse outcome.'

The Bishop coughed.

'The Committee of Academic Correction and Real World Knowledge—hereafter known as C-O-C-K—stipulates you make an apology to fellow staff for having written the book, that you agree to have the books pulped, that you make a donation to the Church, and that you resign from your teaching post without causing any fuss.'

How was he going to live?

'We are, as you know, a tolerant university, guided by spiritual values, and we do not wish you to be without some kind of meaningful employment. The committee has agreed, rather generously I feel, you take on the role of Chief Trolley Man on the University Bliss Train. If you keep your nose clean you might yet reach pensionable age though of course your pension will be much smaller now. You might become,' the Bishop was trying out a jocular tone, 'the man with a pocket full of croissants, or is it currants? Luncheon at the Cannon Street Hotel followed by a weekend at the Metropole. Not that you'll be able to afford to stay in hotels anymore. Incidentally the pension age is seventy-five for low-level workers.'

Dr Philips picked up the pen and signed his name.

'Chief Trolley Man. It could have been a lot worse Dr Philips!'

His viscera were so tightly knotted he could barely breathe.

'Excellent,' said the Bishop. 'You ought to know Professor Leech—in Hong Kong on university business—has sent a recommendation. As an acknowledgement of your interest in all things French he suggests we stock the trolley with Simone De Beauvoir's Lightly Effervescent Water. What do you say to that?'

Chapter Five

ARRY BLINK looked at the ceiling and blinked. He should have been dragging himself out of bed. It was a bed he was paying for on the never-never. You could order beds on the never-never from Shit Town. He'd insisted on a top-of-the-range model, not that a top-of-the-range model on the never-never from Shit Town was particularly nice.

Sunday. Physical exhaustion. Spiritual aridity. Onanism. The new Vice-Chancellor was having her feet massaged, she was already approaching her third climax. The Bishop was kneeling in front of an aubergine, her Shih Tzu puckering its anal glands. The clerks were polishing their lanyards before attending a weekend session of Pilates Plus.

The clerks were the Pontius Pilate Collective, with their spread sheets and bureaucratic sewage, selling education down a foul-smelling river. They listened to Radio Bliss; hours of Dire Straits on an endless loop of mediocrity.

Harry Blink ought to be doing his reflectivity exercises. The Office of Continuous Improvement sent Friday communiqués suggesting weekends were perfect for reflection. Your health and well-being are important to us. We cannot emphasize too much our gratitude for the efforts of colleagues across the Faculty. However there is always room for improvement! The Office of Continuous Improvement suggested additional dog grooming exercises, should one have a dog, or brisk walks—'head up, back straight!'—to the local Co-op, now a franchise of the University.

Harry stepped onto an empty bus heading to the Forest. Tristan wanted to see him and Suki was cooking lunch. Come round. We have some alcohol. He liked Tristan and he liked Suki. She had a black belt in some obscure Martial Art.

Tristan was waiting at the bus stop in a trilby hat. He managed to look almost happy and on those occasions when Tristan managed to look almost happy the world let out a low whistle. They lived in a ramshackle house ten miles from Brackenhurst. They had been granted a permit to live in the Forest because of Suki's American connections. Residents were vetted and given a low surveillance rating, making their lives relatively normal. The house had a garden which slipped down to the heath and in the garden there were several sheds.

There were samizdat magazines and revolutionary tracts in some of them. In others there were plugs, blue leads, red tubes, towers, hubs, cassettes, video players, old Nokias, electronic jammers, blockers, defunct British telecom gadgetry, printers, dial-up phones, turntables, the stuff from skips which had been long been jettisoned for wireless and Blue Tooth Plus, or Red Tiger Claw if you were lucky enough to have a five-star citizen score.

Leads and coils and electronic gadgets twitched and writhed like octopuses slowly coming into life.

After a vegetarian lunch and a smoke, Tristan took a record out of its sleeve and popped it on a record player, circa 1975. *Take me to the river, drop me in the water, take me to the river, push me in the water . . .*

An afternoon sun was breaking through. March was relaxing, the garden was dotted with bashful daffodils.

'Let's take a walk,' Tristan said.

They went through a gate at the back of the garden and made their way along a muddy path, crossed a brook, and reached a wood that had been whipped by winds and chastened by a long winter. There was a couple of deer looking at them with inscrutable curiosity. Harry wondered whether they worked for the authorities.

They walked some more and a shed came into view. Tristan removed a slat of wood and pushed open the door. There was an electric bulb dangling from the ceiling, and there was a standing lamp which gave out a more concentrated light.

'Welcome to the hut,' Tristan said in a German accent, 'my very own Bletchley Park.'

The primitive military computer—circa 1950—sat on a tower and there was something which resembled a ship's wheel held up by pieces of metal and surrounded by tubes and coils, and a bulbous microphone which might have come from a jazz club and a couple of enormous speakers.

'Not exactly state of the art,' said Tristan. 'Yet it's under the radar, *off net*. No chance of anyone tracing anything back to me.'

Harry sat on a plastic chair.

Tristan cranked the wheel and there was a sound like a wind which got louder and louder and the knob turned red and there was a splutter of smoke and a series of muffled, disembodied voices.

Harry said, 'It's like listening to Lord Tennyson on amphetamines.'

Tristan shoved a lead into a socket and the screen flickered with green data and the voices which had been inchoate were becoming clearer. One sounded like Gladys Nirvana and the other sounded like the Bishop. They were laughing.

Tristan cranked more and the voices became louder. One could easily imagine they were doing some kind of dance. And now the words were clear:

> Creative Writing came down the hill,
> carrying with it a bag of swill.
>
> Creative Writing is so exciting.
> After the thunder comes the lightning,
>
> Creative Writing is so inviting
> Creative Writing is Creative Shite-ing
>
> Creative Writing is . . .

Then pop, pop, pop and everything fizzled out.

CHAPTER SIX

ONDAY MORNING, 5.45 AM. Harry Blink PhD was running late. He was running. He got to the Brutalist Central Station feeling hot. He swiped his Bliss Movement Card, elbowing a woman with a Zimmer Frame—she was attending the Commonwealth Zimmer Games—and got on the train before the doors shut. Other than the Zimmer-Framers, one of whom was wearing a track suit top saying NOT DEAD YET, the platform was empty.

The train, however, was not. It was full of academics, poorly paid nurses, care home workers, cleaners, waiters, retail staff, low level data inputters, trainee bureaucrats and anyone who'd voted against the National Alliance Party. Every citizen had a work quota. Every citizen wore a dangling lanyard.

'Welcome to the Bliss Train. This is a non-stop service to the University of Bliss. We will not be stopping at Brackenhurst today. There is an at-seat trolley service, serving yesterday's pretzels.'

Harry realised he'd left his lanyard at home. He was going to get into trouble for that. Professor Leech kept assiduous records in the Lanyard Book.

Harry managed to find two empty seats. He could spread out a bit, close his eyes, listen to Ravel on Blotify. Walter Pater was right;

everything craves musical transfiguration. It takes away the pain or spreads a thick layer of balm over it.

He was teaching an eight o'clock poetry class. Dr Blink had slept badly, consumed by looming disciplinary proceedings, the Shit Town blues, and his neverland bed not yet paid for on the never-never which seemed to have developed a crack in the base in which some rodent was setting up home. Probably on Rinder this very moment, looking for a mate.

Harry hadn't published anything for years other than some recalcitrant paper called 'The Nascent Ill-Being of Wellbeing' which had caused a storm on Witter-Shitter and generated a letter from the Bishop asking whether he had given any thought to the healing power of the Weeping Aubergine. Her door was always open she said, her Shih Tzu ready for a dog-stroking session and why not have a go at clearing up Ethelred's excrement with a poop-zapper for good measure. The exercise would do him good.

Wolves were howling in Romanian forests. They were howling in Scotland too, now they'd been reintroduced into that newly independent country. Some were crossing the border like Auden's mail train, loping south. One of Harry's students had written a poem called 'Shutter-Fuck! Shutter-Fuck! Shutter-Fuck!'

His Sunday with Tristan and Suki had been instructive. There was a strange, almost unrecognisable feeling buried deep down in his entrails. In an earlier period of his life he would have recognised it as hope. It was dangerous to entertain that feeling in 2035.

Tristan's Bletchley Park! A chink of light. A way of outwitting the university's surveillance apparatus. Of being one step ahead. Intel. He had shared his thoughts about the deer with Tristan and his colleague had put his hand on Harry's shoulder in a brotherly way: 'Don't worry, I can tell if a deer is a deer or some AI installation.'

Tristan had been working on his off-net computer for years. He called it the Blake Programme. If he wasn't resurrecting octopuses with electronic currents he was foraging berries, popping mushrooms and reciting Basho to the birds.

Harry trusted Tristan, and he trusted Suki. There was Humph too. A loose cannon sponsored by the International Lacanian Movement. This hadn't prevented him from winning the International Leonora Carrington Prize.

Tristan and Suki had spoken to Harry in confidence—often in the Forest, over drunken lunches and suppers—and although Suki never spelt anything out it was clear in Harry's mind she'd worked for the CIA and had a knowledge of espionage that was complemented by her skills in the kitchen and the elegant kimonos she wore at their clandestine poetry readings.

Tristan's apparent amateurishness—the broken pieces of a computer were like a poem in need of several more drafts—was matched by Suki's knowledge of software. They had explained to Harry, tactfully, without loading him with too much information, they were working on the Blake Resistance Programme.

Just to say 'William Blake' made you feel better.

Not only was Tristan a forager of fruits and a collector of hardware he was good at collecting information on the move. He was no slouch with a g-phone, surreptitiously recording and filming Black Hole Wild-Fi Spots on a campus packed with CCTV.

'Be like tumbleweed,' Suki liked to say.

She taught him how to outwit Facial Recognition. Wearing a latex glove he imprinted biological auditory spores in semiotic spaces—university signage, non-binary lavatory doors, library Wob Tops—and late at night, after an evening postgrad class, he found his way to the roof of the New Building and smeared a receptor trace ver Our Lady of the Aubergines, an act of sacrilege which could have got him a life sentence in Shit Town.

Suki hacked beautifully. She could call in a favour and have the latest micro drone fly above the university with stealth, sucking up data, capturing images, film footage, synchronising with the visual auditory spores planted by Tristan. Back in the Forest they studied the findings over a glass of bourbon.

The new Vice-Chancellor was relaxing in her office, feet on the desk, and sitting on the other side was Professor Leech who was removing her shoes and massaging her toes with dedication. The Vice-Chancellor threw back her head and moaned like Cicciolina. Here was Fred Clueless burning books behind the library. And Ms Grogan, two Wow Techs to her name, ought to be more careful. She'd left a receipt on the passenger seat of her sports car which showed she'd been using the University Gold Plus Expenses Card to buy high end sex toys which came from a bespoke dealer in Bucharest. Professor Penelope Peacock spent most of the time playing with her Lego set, thereby earning her large salary. And who were those men in suits and dark glasses stepping out of a black limousine behind The Fairly Old Building speaking on their Q-phones? Could that be Annunziata Kumquat, the Home Secretary?

The drone had done a good job on the Bishop.

Tristan lit a joint and Suki pushed the amplification button.

Imelda had set up a triptych of aubergines on a Reni Macintosh table and lit a candle and then with ritualistic deliberation she knelt on the floor, next to her Shih Tzu, and put her hands together, her lips moving in silent prayer and then, as if seized by the drug of love, she threw herself on the ground, her head almost touching the table, the trinity of aubergines blinking in some kind of electronic display. Ethelred cocked a leg.

'Such fervour,' Tristan said, blowing out a spiral of weed.

Footage showed Imelda talking to her dog. She spoke quietly: 'You know I love you dearly Ethel and you are my most favourite Shih Tzu in the whole wide world.' The dog moved its head with a look of sadness. 'Every now and again,' continued the Bishop, 'I need to wire you up to my Wob Top Super Plus just to check you really are top of the range. I know you don't like it dear but the literature says it's a painless procedure, or at least only a little uncomfortable, and that seems to depend on how much I turn up the Discombobulation Dial. And there's hardly any point having a dial if you can't see how far it goes.'

The dog made a strange human sound. 'The thing is,' Imelda continued, 'you're not a gimmick are you? I'm testing your communication-algorithm potentiality and it might be that I can tap in a pedagogical programme which would give you the power to speak and just think what that would mean!'

A Gregorian chant started up on the Divinity Line. She pushed the dog out of the way away and got into Teresa of Avila mode. If she'd been a dog she would have cocked her leg too but she was a Bishop consumed by a gnostic fire.

CHAPTER SEVEN

'LIGHT REFRESHMENTS, sandwiches, lovely lovely short bread, croissants, pretzels, hot drinks, Simone de Beauvoir's Lightly Effervescent Water . . .' The trolley man was pushing his trolley down the aisles. He looked as if he'd been given electroshock therapy.

Since his demotion to Trolley Man, Philips had retreated behind his shell. Harry tried to coax him into conversation, catching glimpses of that once creative mind. That was before the Office of Continuous Improvement got their claws into him. They'd lowered his citizenship score and given him a room in Shirley Towers. He said he was working on the Marquis de Sade. An odd choice for such a mild man but nowadays Sadeian realities were a train journey away.

'I should have been a Juliette rather than a Justine,' he said on one occasion.

Harry asked for a bottle of Simone de Beauvoir's Lightly Effervescent Water. He had the taste of cigarettes in his mouth, and he wanted to wash the taste away. Philips handed him a glass with some ice and a slice of lemon. The water was usually pleasant but today it was vile.

The teaching staff, lanyards around their necks, their PhDs propping up boxes of cauliflowers in the Food Bank, walked past Trollop Towers and on through the graveyard.

Harry had a reoccurring dream. He was tied to a bed in a Swiss clinic. The clinicians had welded a metal colander onto his head. Through the holes they had inserted surgical straws which pushed into the top of the brain. Anything of value was sucked out.

'We will have finished soon,' the doctor said. 'Though we'd like you to come back in six months' time.'

Dr O'Flaherty, history lecturer, one of a dwindling few, started singing 'It's such a perfect day' and the corpses under the earth stretched and yawned and thanked the Lord they'd escaped this new world order.

Harry stepped into Room Wow-Wow 17.

There were thirty students in the class, and it was quieter than the graveyard. Students were looking at their g-phones; some of the wealthier ones had acquired Q-phones. No one spoke and there was a vague feeling of hostility. They had begun to realise they'd spend their lives paying back their university fees.

Dr Blink's eight o'clock class was Pop Up Poetry. Each module was required to demonstrate its employability value otherwise the module was pulled. Harry along with his colleagues spent much of the summer grappling with flow charts showing the monetary value of former students who had attended their courses. Harry thought the point of poetry was that it released you from having to undertake any meaningful employment but he knew if he said that he would be in Shit Town for a three month taster. He pointed out that several poets in the past had worked as spies but this caused a crisis meeting with Senior Management and a phone call to the Home Secretary which resulted in Dr Blink being reprimanded for his cavalier handling of the facts. The Dean intimated there could be a disciplinary proceeding if he didn't expunge the information from the Employability Report ASAP.

'What about Basil Bunting?' Harry asked.

'I don't give a shit about Basil Bunting,' the Dean said.

The Bishop had a more sentimental view. She had enjoyed poetry with the Sisters of Mercy. The more talented girls were allowed to look at devotional lyrics. Imelda had given a paper at the Great Theological Conference in North Town. T.S Eliot, she argued, had made numerous references to the aubergine which could be traced back to ancient Sanskrit texts. Accordingly the lines

> O the moon shone bright on Mrs. Porter
> And on her daughter
> They wash their feet in soda water

alluded to irrigation techniques carried out by female priests in which the fertilisation of the aubergine not only expressed the procurement of life in a practical sense but which also acted as an overarching metaphor for the parched soul. Soda water was an outward sign of inward grace.

And Senior Management noted financial institutions often larded their publicity with poetic jingles or employed some youthful poet to look meaningfully at the camera and argue in rhyme that money made the world go round which was good for everybody, especially those with money.

'Today,' said Dr Blink, 'we're going to look at a poem by Sylvia Plath.' He was skating on thin ice. Last year one of his students—Izzy perhaps? or was it Hermione?—had run out the room. God, thought Dr Blink, now what? Soon enough Roxanna Grogan sent a doomail saying there had been a complaint. Why did poetry have to be so horrible? There were lots of nice things in the world Dr Blink, small animals, hot water bottles, butterflies. Why not set up a business relationship with a card-making company and get the students to write birthday wishes and anniversary cards? Here, she explained, they could do rhymes and earn some money at the same time. Good for his Employability Report too. You need to think outside the box Dr Blink, she added. On this occasion Harry pretended he hadn't received the doomail but the Dean had followed up by saying he didn't want to hear of any more students running out of poetry classes because their emotions had been stirred up.

'Has anyone heard of Sylvia Plath?' Harry asked.

Thirty pairs of financially indebted eyeballs studied him for a moment. No one answered. Harry wondered whether the question had insulted their intelligence. This could go either way.

'She was quite famous,' he continued, as if this were an afterthought. Keep it simple he reminded himself. 'She married an English poet called Ted Hughes who wrote a lot of poems about foxes, crows, that kind of stuff—back in the day.'

A girl at the back put her hand up.

'Beth, any thoughts?'

'Was she the one who put her head in a gas oven?'

'I think you're onto something.' There was an uncomfortable silence.

'Dr Blink, do you know why she put her head in a gas oven?' The question came from a young woman who had never spoken before.

Harry didn't recognise her. She had a European accent. Harry put his hand on his chin. 'It certainly wasn't an accident. In fact, I don't think she was in a happy place,' he started rambling. 'You have to remember the winter of 1963 was one of the worst on record and there wasn't any central heating in those days . . .'

'When was 1963?' asked Zac. Harry wondered whether his question was a leg break tossed disingenuously into the air. If he went too far down the pitch he might get stumped.

'1963,' said Dr Blink, 'let's say, was quite emphatically not 1962 and neither was it yet 1964.'

There was a ripple of laughter and Zac looked pissed off. Damn, he'll be making a complaint too if I'm not careful and, in an attempt to rescue the situation, Harry went on to say '1963 was the year Kennedy was assassinated.'

The silence continued.

Clever Maurice put his hand up. 'Who was that French poet who took his pet lobster to the gardens of the Palais Royal?'

'Oh yes,' Harry said, surprised he could remember, 'that was Gérard de Nerval. He hanged himself from a lamppost.'

Why on earth did he say that?! It was too early in the morning. It was impossible to think clearly, never mind teach Pop Up Poetry to a bunch of students who'd been neutralised by corporate values even before they were conceived.

'What happened to the lobster?'

'Ended up as a Lobster Thermidor, I believe.'

Maurice was warming to the theme, if there were a theme. 'Would you say poets had an unusual propensity for self-immolation?'

'Would you like to explain that phrase to the class Maurice?'

The almost likeable boy tossed his head back and said in a fake American accent 'Err it means checking out early.'

The girl with the European accent, blonde and pale, said 'Leaving without paying the bill?'

Harry had to agree that poets did sometimes leave without paying the bill.

Maurice said, 'Have you thought of checking out early Dr Blink?'

'That's a rather challenging question at 8.20 in the morning Maurice.'

Mind you, not an altogether unreasonable question, Harry wanted to add.

The class looked interested for once. After twenty years of teaching Harry realised the teacher was the clown with a disproportionately large nose who scared the children and made the parents laugh. For a moment Harry thought of lovely things: As cool as the pale wet leaves of lily-of-the-valley, he said to himself, she lay beside me.

'If you turn to page thirteen in the Touch Me Now Reading Pack,' he continued, 'you'll find Plath's poem "Daddy".'

He could imagine Roxana Grogan at her desk shooting off doomails with zest, especially as she might not have disentangled herself from that big-eared Romanian Rabbit she'd bought from Bucharest.

'I ought to say from the beginning that "Daddy" is a disturbing poem and there's a lot of holocaustic imagery.' As an afterthought, he added 'Not the sort of poem you'd send your father on Father's Day.'

The only thing Harry received in the post were the details of forthcoming disciplinary hearings.

Several students were now writing notes. As he watched them scribbling away Dr Blink found himself thinking 'Daddy' was no less disturbing than the University of Bliss.

'Is it a metaphor?' asked Maurice.

'The aubergine?'

'What aubergine?' said the boy.

'Is it a metaphor?' asked Maurice again.

'Most things are metaphors I suppose. I mean, I don't think many women are fond of fascists. Mussolini did have a lot of female admirers though.'

Somebody asked who Mussolini was. Harry chose to ignore the question and carried on with his introduction to the poem.

'There are some personal details too. Plath's father was a university lecturer who would have stood at a black board, just as I am doing now, only it's not a black board is it? It's a Wob Wob Screen. And Otto Plath died when Sylvia was eight.'

Someone shouted 'You mean ten. It says ten in the poem—"I was ten when they buried you." '

'I know it does,' said Blink, 'but actually she was eight.'

'She was fibbing then?'

'There's something we call poetic truth, and in any case ten sounds better than eight, doesn't it? It sort of alliterates with "twenty" as in "At twenty I tried to die and get back, back, back to you".'

'She wasn't happy,' Lizzy said.

Maurice said, 'Did Otto Plath check out early?'

'He just died I think.'

'Because he was a Nazi?'

'He died Maurice. He died. It's difficult to work out whether he was a Nazi or not—I don't think he was a Nazi in the absolute sense. He was an entomologist. He wrote *Bumble Bees and their Ways.*'

'I love bumble bees,' Zac said.

Maurice had the wind in his sails. He pointed out that Plath must have had an Electra Complex.

'Would you like to explain that to the class Maurice?'

'It's the opposite of an Oedipal Complex.'

Beth said, 'What's that Dr Blink?'

'You know—Oedipus killed his father because he wanted to sleep with his mother and was afraid his father was going to castrate him.'

There was the sound of a moving chair and a theatrical sigh and to his alarm Harry looked up to see Tulip Jackson, sometimes known as Jackson Tulip, his promising non-binary student, making their way to the door and the class was reduced to twenty-nine.

This isn't good, Harry thought.

'I think Tulip's upset,' said Beth.

'I think you mean Jackson,' Megan whispered conspiratorially.

'Yes,' Harry said, 'I shouldn't have mentioned Oedipus. I shouldn't have said anything at all. I should have stood next to the Wob Wob Screen and juggled balls in the air.' Whatever you say, say nothing, he said to himself, remembering Seamus Heaney's sensible advice.

The class looked worried.

Harry blinked and continued, 'When you read through 'Daddy' you'll notice a persistent jagged-y rhyme scheme, almost a nursery rhyme if you will.' The students liked rhyme. 'And there is a rapid, though not entirely incongruous movement, from concentration camps to vampires.'

He'd used the V word which sent shudders of excitement through his students as their minds flitted from Harry Potter—still churned out in depressingly large numbers in 2035—to the latest drama on Get Flicks—I Suck Your Blood And You Suck Mine.

'I wonder if anyone would like to read the poem? A volunteer?'

This was the moment when silence descended like a funeral parlour waiting for the corpse and Harry would gear up to read the poem himself, a poem he'd read many times, which still sent a jolt of electricity through his desiccated brain. He looked up once more in case he might the catch the face of Maurice or Beth or Izzy, like an auctioneer pausing before banging down the hammer. No one has stepped up to the plate. Get your reading voice ready Dr Blink.

'Please, I want to read "Daddy", said the blonde with the European accent.

Harry looked at the girl. 'Thank you,' he said, and again 'thank you . . .'

'Magda,' she said, 'my name's Magda'.

'Thank you, Magda.'

She breathed deeply and began:

> You do not do, you do not do
> Anymore, black shoe
> In which I have lived like a foot
> For thirty years, poor and white,
> Barely daring to breathe or Achoo.

She read well, hardly stumbling over words and transforming mispronunciations into magnificent flourishes and relaying a charge when she got to 'My Polack friend says / there are a dozen or two. / So I never could tell / where you put your foot, your root' and 'I thought every German was you and the language obscene' and 'I began to talk like a Jew. / I think I may well be a Jew' and 'I have always been scared of *you*, / With your Luftwaffe, your gobbledygoo.' And she read the final verse with brio:

> There's a stake in your fat black heart
> And the villagers never liked you.
> They are dancing and stamping on you.
> They always knew it was you.
> Daddy, daddy, you bastard, I'm through.

There was a different kind of silence now. A good silence. Maurice started clapping as did Beth, Ben, Amy, Lizzy, Izzy, Milly, Molly, Poppy, Hermione, Matt, Dulcea . . . If only Tulip Jackson and/or Jackson Tulip would come back and throw some non-binary clapping into the mix. Nine o'clock in the morning and his Pop-Up Poetry class was clapping! Heartfelt clapping at that and Harry noticed a little blood was putting colour into Magda's cheeks. Put that in your Employability Report Professor Leech, Panzer man Panzer man.

There was a knock on the door and the Dean's head poked into the room. 'Dr Blink, there's seems to be a lot of noise in here.'

'Poetry appreciation Professor Leech.'

If Leech had had a pot he would have pissed in it.

'I believe you have a break at midday. I'd like a word in my office. Twelve o'clock sharp. Remember your punctuality ratings, they're not very good at the moment.'

CHAPTER EIGHT

A T ELEVEN FORTY-FIVE in the morning Harry made his way to the Crimson Building, formerly known as the Faculty of Arts. Thanks to Imelda's procurement of funds from the Light of Idaho the university was embracing the colour purple, or some variation of that colour, across the campus, as if a cardinal were laying out his purple smalls on the steps of the Vatican. The church was spreading its aesthetic into every nook and cranny—into every nook and fanny, quipped Humph in a French accent. Even the blackbirds had acquired a maroon tinge.

Leech thought the Church of the Aubergine was bunkum but he knew which side his bread was buttered on and it gave him another excuse to harass the staff. If they avoided dog stroking sessions, Polyamorous Cake Baking or Spiritually Enriching Customer Service Workshops he could drag them in.

When a young English lecturer (Staff Study Buddy Number 73) threw himself off Trollop Towers it came to light he hadn't reached his annual quota of dog stroking sessions and he hadn't attended the recent Growth Mindset Seminar nor had he gone on the campus Tree Walk and neither had he signed up for the compulsory Menstruation Awareness Seminar and he'd certainly not signed up for that online course 'How to Use the Mandala Stones in the Work

Place'. When the union brought up the question of his workload the university was exonerated because they had provided every opportunity for their staff to develop their wellbeing and on this occasion, sadly, the deceased member of staff had chosen not to avail himself of the university's Five Star Programme. Not only was the said person now dead, he was posthumously reprimanded for not having toed the line.

Roxana Grogan wanted a disciplinary proceeding but the Bishop pointed out that this would be complicated because Dr Jones had already been cremated. To make herself feel better she whipped out the University Gold Plus Expenses Card and checked out the latest offers from Bucharest.

Professor Leech could see that Imelda's church stuff, if carefully managed behind the scenes, strengthened his position. His salary was bumped up every year and every time he sacked a member of staff he got a cash bonus. His discovery that Vice-Chancellor Nirvana had a foot fetish meant he had a constant boner.

When the teaching staff wrote Annual Wellbeing Reports they had to demonstrate how the values of the institution informed their research, not that they had any time for research. Anything to do with dog welfare attracted a generous grant. Everyone knew what had happened to Dr Philips and there were rumours of dissenting lecturers being bundled into university vans and unceremoniously dumped in the malodorous outskirts of Shit Town.

The walk to Leech's panopticon office was never pleasant. Harry found himself rehearsing the many things he might have done wrong. Tulip, aka Jackson, had probably lodged a complaint and the fact he hadn't got his lanyard was going to give the Dean even more ammunition. It would be ironic if at the very moment he's almost paid for his top of the range bed from Shit Town he ended up being re-located there. Harry had to walk past several administrators gloating with schadenfreude. They could see he had been summoned to the Dean's office. No one made that journey through the Crimson Building voluntarily. It was about time that useless poet got his comeuppance.

The nice new administrator, whose niceness would be knocked out of her soon enough, liked quoting 'Not Waving But Drowning'. She gave him a compassionate look. Her kindly eyes seemed to say all the dog stroking sessions in the world won't sweeten this university cauchemar.

'Come,' said the Dean after Harry had knocked on the door at twelve o'clock precisely and before he had time to compose himself Dr Blink was sitting on the other side of Leech's desk watching a retro-modern executive toy: steel balls in a Newtonian cradle trapped in a relentless gravitational pull. Were they the testicles of Dr Jones encased in a metallic shell smacking against each other in a metronomic hell?

The Dean had an African Grey. When he'd learnt about the Pro-Vice-Chancellor's acquisition of the Shih Tzu he'd put in a request for a top of the range parrot. The former Vice-Chancellor had agreed on condition it was the cheaper middle range model. The Bishop didn't like this at first but came round to the idea when she realised the parrot was a talker.

After ten minutes of metronomic ball-smacking the parrot shrieked 'Ten minutes! Ten minutes!'

He was a busy man. Professor Leech liked to haul in his staff and kick them out as quickly as possible. Today the Dean was dressed in the colours of a Jesuit, a man in black with a *Mein Kampf* look, of meagre build whose face, sometimes bearded, sometimes not, habitually snarled at the world. Harry reckoned he had a short man complex and guessed the Dean must have undergone vowel stretching exercises because his Birmingham accent had been almost entirely squeezed out resulting in a voice of graceless functionality.

'Dr Blink, I won't beat around the bush. You're a waste of space. I think I've told you before that if it weren't for the Pro-Vice-Chancellor, I'd have re-located you to Shit Town before you could say colonic irrigation. Plato was right about poets, if anything he was too generous.'

One of the university's purple vans might be parked outside Harry's flat right now. A couple of porters dismantling his bed and throwing his paltry belongings out of the window.

'The only reason I let you teach poetry is that Imelda has some ridiculously quaint idea it's good for the soul. Whose soul I don't know, certainly not mine which doesn't need any fucking poetry in it. And for the time being, for reasons I can't fathom either, students continue to sign up for it. Once that stops you're toast, whatever the Bishop says.'

'I suppose,' he continued with a degree of resignation, 'there was that student who got that gig on TV Plus selling Stanley Morgan Financial Services using a rather catchy rhyme. You should try and make that happen more often Dr Blink. Money tastes better than honey—You can't argue with that.'

Harry remembered Basil Bunting's 'What the Chairman Told Tom':

> Nasty little words, nasty long words,
> it's unhealthy.
> I want to wash when I meet a poet.
>
> They're Reds, addicts,
> all delinquents.
> What you write is rot.

Dr Blink had suffered the Dean's snarl on many occasions. The Dean had a neurological dislike of other people's voices. Unless he were with one of the two women who ran the university, and then he became a smiling toad.

'What the fuck's "poetry" anyway?'

In other circumstances this might have been a philosophical question.

'Poetry is imaginary gardens with real *crapeux* in them,' Harry said.

'I always knew there was a lot of crappo.'

The Newtonian balls continued to clack.

'What was the last thing you published?'

'*The Street of Perfect Love.*'

'Oh lord I looked at that recently just to see how crap it was. I'm looking at your online CV Dr Blink and it says you published that thing in 2018. That's seventeen years ago. Prolific aren't you? What an absurdly pretentious title. You should have called it *The Street of Perfect Shite.*'

The Dean referred to his own publications at length: *The Craft of Management Part One*, *The Craft of Management Part Two* and the much acclaimed *Small Is Good, Smaller is Even Better.* He told Harry he was now working on something 'world leading'.

'Someone's got to do some work around here,' he added.

No point reminding the Dean he spent his time writing Reflectivity Reports, Action Plans, attending Compliancy Workshops, delivering papers at Lego Play and Creativity Symposia, not to mention teaching classes round the clock and grading student work which however badly written could never be failed.

'Do you know how many copies of that shitty pamphlet you sold?'

'It wasn't a best seller.'

'Spot on there! According to my Wob Top Analytica survey it sold one hundred and fifty copies!'

'I believe it's out of print.'

'Should never have been in print.'

The parrot shrieked 'Ten Minutes! Ten Minutes!' for the second time.

'Do you know how many copies of *Pure Reflectivity* the Vice-Chancellor has shifted?'

'More than a hundred and fifty copies.'

'Come, come, Dr Blink no need to state the obvious. Gladys has sold,' he looked again at the screen, 'eight hundred thousand copies and rising. What do you say to that?'

'Extraordinary,' Harry said.

'Incidentally Blink, what's happened to your lanyard?'

'I left it at home I think.'

'Think?' If you've left it somewhere else that could be a violation of data security. You'll get it in the neck for that, I can tell you.'

'It's at home Professor.'

'South Town?' asked Leech.

'Yes, South Town.'

'How does Shit Town sound Dr Blink? '

'Awful.'

'Let that thought hover in the air as I write your name in the Lanyard Book. Not the first time is it? You're something of a recidivist.'

Harry watched him write with great care *Dr Blink came to the campus without a lanyard, 25 March, 2035,—again.*

The Dean looked pleased with himself. 'An interesting morning hey?' He tossed Harry a bunch of spreadsheets. They showed the earning power of former students who'd done his poetry modules. 'Not good are they?' the Dean said with satisfaction.

The parrot raised its wings, thrust out its beak and shrieked: 'I am not Flaubert's Parrot! I am the Dean's Parrot! I am not Flaubert's Parrot! I am the Dean's Parrot!'

It hovered above the table next to Leech's desk spreading its wings, swivelling itself round like a mechanical toy. Then it fired a streak of shit which zapped the Dean's jacket, and then it did it again.

'Fucking parrot!' The Dean leapt up and snatched a box of tissues and tried to wipe the gunk off his clothes. His shirt and trousers hadn't escaped. 'Fucking hopeless middle of the range my arse parrot!'

'He must have bought it on the University Gold Plus Expenses Card,' Harry said to himself.

'You're *not* supposed to spray *me* with that shit!' Leech took another tissue and tried to wipe the green mess off, not realising he was making it a lot worse.

Dr Blink sat impassively, straining to keep a straight face.

'I'd rather you didn't look at me like that,' said the Dean, beetroot coloured.

Harry wondered whether Suki had hacked into the parrot's Shooter Poot.

The Dean leant forward; his face alarmingly close to Harry's 'If this ever gets out you're going to be a lifelong resident of Shit Town. Understood?'

'Who would I tell?' said Harry.

The Dean looked at him suspiciously.

Harry continued: 'Mind you, it would be very generous of you if my lanyard violation were expunged.'

The Dean scratched his head, took his pen and ostentatiously put a line through the sentence he'd just written in The Lanyard Book.

'On this occasion,' said the Dean, 'I shall overlook your bare-arsed cheek.'

He closed The Lanyard Book with a bang.

The parrot lay on its back, black tongue lolling out, spent. The Newtonian ball-clack petered out. There was an unpleasant smell in the room. The Dean opened a drawer and pulled out a bottle of deodorant. He walked around the office, his arm above his head spraying indiscriminately.

'I'll be back.'

He walked out of the office, closed the door, and locked it behind him. The Dean had locked him in with a comatose parrot. He'd never been locked in the Dean's office. There was a clock on the wall and he watched the minute hand judder. The parrot started to make a clicking noise. Seven minutes, nine minutes, it seemed an age and Harry got up and started walking around the office. The bookshelf had multiple copies of the Dean's books on managerial craft and there was a signed copy of *Pure Reflectivity*. He put it back in case the Dean walked in.

'Leechy, my office door is always open,' it said. 'Gladys Nirvana, VC.'

He stood a moment behind the Dean's chair and saw that his Super Wob was open. Doomails were bouncing in as he looked.

One from the VC said, 'Shall we get rid of Creative Shite-ing altogether?'

Harry slid back into his chair and heard a key in the lock. Leech was wearing a new jacket, a new shirt and a new pair of trousers. He'd splashed himself with a generous amount of cologne.

'Right,' his tone had changed, 'let's get down to business Dr Blink.'

Leech must have changed in the room which said No Person May Enter Here and taken the opportunity to spy on Harry via CCTV.

Thank goodness he hadn't sat in the Dean's chair and made the universal hand gesture of the professional wanker.

'Professor Nirvana will soon be making her inaugural lecture as Professor of Entomology and new Vice-Chancellor. Her lecture is entitled The Nascent Hexapod. You will have seen the notices around the campus.'

'I didn't know we had a Department of Entomology.'

The VC's working on it.'

'Excellent,' said Harry.

The Dean looked at him quizzically. 'I didn't know you were interested in entomology.'

'Lucretius, *De Rerum Natura*, it's all there.'

The Dean didn't deign to ask who Lucretius was. He didn't give a shit.

'You will have noticed how she's shaken up the place. There's a buzz in the air, don't you think? Employees wear their lanyard with greater pride, present company excluded. Insider information indicates we've risen ten places up the League Table, it's not official yet.'

'So we are in eightieth position?' Harry said.

'That's not the point. In a year's time we will be pushing even higher. The university is punching above its weight. And there are plans in the pipeline, Dr Blink. Big plans. I'm giving you a chance to redeem yourself.'

Harry could see that the Dean had missed some shit on the arm of his chair.

'The inaugural lecture is a cause for celebration. Anybody who's anybody will be there. We expect a hundred percent attendance on the part of the staff. I have a job for you—one which you should be more than happy to accept.' He paused and looked Harry in the eye. 'I want you to write a poem.'

'I thought you didn't like poems.'

'I fucking hate them but this is different because I'm commissioning the poem and you are being commissioned, not that you'll get any money for it. I expect we could give you a 20-pound hat voucher for the next Play and Creativity Festival.'

'Better than a slap round the face with a wet fish,' said Dr Blink. But it wasn't better at all.

'The *Chronicle* will be there of course. An excellent marketing occasion for the university. Your poem better be good—in praise of VC Nirvana.' The Dean's pasty cheeks were reddening.

'The iguana,' Harry whispered.

'What?'

'I coughed.'

'Didn't sound like a cough to me. Did you say iguana?'

'That does rhyme with Nirvana.'

'Which is why I asked whether you said it, you fool!'

'Wish I had. It's a good rhyme. Nirvana, Iguana.'

'Listen Blink, my parrot can hear everything. I could just ask it to repeat what you said. We don't want to discover you are a liar as well as a persistent forgetter of lanyards. Do you want me to ask the parrot?'

'It might shit on you again.'

The Dean scowled. Harry could see he was weighing up the possibility. Leech would be in touch with the Nigerian Parrot Company later that day. Harry could see the parrot had regained its vertical position and was loading up.

'You'd better start work on this today. Take that fucking iguana out for a start. I want you to make sure you get in the following—make a note. Quickly now.'

Dr Blink took out a notebook.

'Ready? Good. League Table, Fiscal Rectitude, Compliancy, Entomology, Pure Reflectivity, Spiritual Doo Dah'—the Dean thought
he'd better get some of that in to please the Bishop—'and I'd like
you to use the phrase Crucible of Change. I like that—Crucible of
Change. Brilliant, isn't it? *Crucible of Change.*'

'I see,' said Dr Blink, who realised he couldn't really walk away
from the job.

'I don't want any of that free verse bollocks either. Playing tennis
without a net. Frost was right about that.

'Questions? Good, well you can go and make a start and please
make sure you wear your lanyard the whole fucking time, ideally
you should wear it at home too, and wear it with pride for fuck's sake.
And the parrot incident didn't happen. Never happened. Wouldn't
happen. Couldn't happen. Got it? I want to see a draft of that poem
ASAP. Now go, Dr Blink. Go!'

The African Grey said in a strangely seductive French voice: 'I
am not Flaubert's parrot. I am the Dean's parrot.'

CHAPTER NINE

BLINK STARTED 'The Crucible of Change' the following day. By writing the title of the poem the words would come. That was the plan. It was a long while since Harry had written a poem. He'd had 'poem thoughts' but they remained just that—thoughts. In any case the unwritten poem was almost certainly the better poem—'It looks well on the page, but never well enough.'

For several days he wrote 'The Crucible of Change' at the top of a blank page.

Sometimes he put the title in capital letters:

THE CRUCIBLE OF CHANGE

Or he played around with the font:

THE CRUCIBLE OF CHANGE

He began to realise the blank page *was* the poem. When the moment came he would say the title—in a BBC voice, circa 1950—The Crucible of Change—and make mouth movements as if he were a fish: O for Omega, O for Oh. The Tristan Tzara of the fishpond. One of his students was working on a poem called 'Screaming into the Void' whilst another was half way through a poem called 'Pissing into the Void', which sounded more fun.

The crucible is irreducible, the crucible is Lucifer-al.

Shostakovich's 'Leningrad' Symphony would play in the background.

Several days later, having re-read Ginsberg for a forthcoming class, he managed to get down the following:

> The lamb stew of the imagination/A lost battalion of platonic conversationalists/All drained of brilliance in the drear light of Zoo—
>
> Who walked alone through the streets of Idaho seeking lachrymose eggplants which were lachrymose eggplants /Seeking jazz or soup or sex or gynaecology, sociology,
>
> applied psychology, entomology—
>
> The heterosexual dollar, the homosexual dollar, the LGBTQ-IAYK[-INK -]Z± dollar, the non-binary trans-friendly intersex dollar. Dollar dollar dollar. (Give me a dollar.
>
> Why? Just fuck off, will you) Where is the next whisky bar? Where is it? Where is it?
>
> (Note to self: throw in a hallelujah? Put a line through this and start again?)

Hallelujah—now move straight to Leonard Cohen. Remember him? His music wasn't played anymore and no one read Cohen's *Beautiful Losers*. Harry found it in a charity shop on the Mutant Mile. It was described on the back as 'the most revolting book ever written in Canada'. The main character was Catherine Tekakwitha. She was a seventeenth century virgin and later she became a saint.

He wrote WELCOME TO THE UNIVERSITY OF BEAUTIFUL LOSERS!

From the beginning of Cohen's novel, mostly for the hell of it, he copied this:

CATHERINE TEKAKWITHA, who are you? Are you (1656–1680)? Is that enough? Are you the Iroquois Virgin? Are you the Lily of the Shores of the Mohawk River? Can I love you in my own way? I am an old scholar, better-looking now than when I was young. That's what sitting on your ass does to your face. I've come after you, Catherine Tekakwitha. I want to know what goes on under that rosy blanket. [. . .] Could you teach me about leaves? Do you know anything about narcotic mushrooms? [. . .] Can an old scholar find love at last and stop having to pull himself off every night so he can get some sleep?

Dr Blink carried on reading 'the most revolting book ever written in Canada' and from Cohen's novel added to his jottings: 'Find a little saint and fuck her over and over in some pleasant part of heaven, get right into her plastic altar.'

If the university found out Harry Blink was reading an experimental 1960s novel there would be the mother of disciplinary hearings. He might be demoted to Assistant Trolley Man.

CHAPTER TEN

GET YOURSELF to the Forest!

It had been a while since Harry had seen Tristan, other than the exchanging of sonnets on the train, and a couple of brief conversations in the corridor of the Crimson Building. There were surveillance cameras everywhere now. The safest option was to meet in the Gender-Neutral Lavatories.

The union had taken out a landmark case against the university for putting cameras in 'Personal Spaces' and on this occasion the union won. The ruling got into got into the *Chronicle*. The Bishop thought there might be a privacy issue.

'Our staff should be able to piss in peace,' she said with unexpected fervour and Roxana Grogan came down on the side of the union too. She used the Gender-Neutral Lavatories to test run her Romanian gadgets.

Leech retreated on this one, pissed off. At least the new parrot had arrived. The Nigerian Parrot Company had agreed on a five-year cost-free extension plan for their Top of the Range All-Hearing All-Shrieking Model, sending a thousand Nigerian apologies for the damage done, and for loss of face. The marketing team in Lagos laughed themselves silly and they spent several days trying out the long-range shitting potentiality of the latest model, whilst listening to Fela Kuti's hit 'Expensive Shit.' By 2035 enshittification was marching across the globe. The Parrot Company offered a bespoke laundry service to ensure the Dean's jacket would be better than new. 'Top of the Range Parrot had several special features too! We are sure you'll be enchanted by it,' wrote Dr Moses Good-Luck, the CEO of the Nigerian Parrot Company.

Tristan and Harry sat in neighbouring booths and passed bits of paper through the gap. They'd developed a flushing code. Two flushes meant caution, three flushes game on. On one occasion they had to sit in silence whilst Grogan spoke to her Romanian contact: 'Fifteen orgasms a week is more than I can cope with.'

Harry took the empty bus to the Forest. The driver looked exactly the same, always the same un-readable face even though he had a tattoo on his neck which said BEAUTIFUL. No smiling. There wasn't much to smile about in 2035 whether you were a robot or not.

Tristan's trilby hat. A whistling sound which was almost happy. The magnolia trees in the garden. Suki hugged Harry and they went into the house with its shabby sofas and lopsided bookshelves, and the smell of cooking wafting from the kitchen.

'You good with a Korean veg curry?' called out Suki in that lovely American voice.

Over lunch they brought up the subject of Stinker Rogers and Larry Lomax. 'Did you know either of them?' Suki asked.

'I never really knew Larry Lomax but I met Stinker Rogers a few times. He was a decent guy. I followed his TV series on archaeological digs.'

'Funny how you can't get hold of it for love nor money. *Dig Deep for Blissfordshire* has disappeared like Rogers himself,' Suki said.

'A hell of a fuss. The police were here,' Tristan continued. 'They know the Forest's a favourite place for suicides and they asked us to keep an eye out for bodies. We found one hanging on a sycamore tree. A cleaner from the university. They'd sacked her for leaving a note on the VC's desk begging for a pay rise. She was a single mum with three children. The university offered 'spiritual counselling' and a special voucher for the cleaners' food bank. All they had were bottles of bleach and a box of marigolds. She drank the bleach and hanged herself. You can be sure that didn't get in the *Chronicle*. They told her kids she'd gone to France, the ultimate disgrace. The children were put in some institution outside Shit Town. I wonder how many people have disappeared from the campus?' Tristan rolled his fist into a ball and flicked out his fingers. Puff . . .

'Stinker Rogers disappeared. Perhaps he got moved to Shit Town?' Harry said.

'We've made enquiries,' said Suki, 'no evidence he fetched up there.'

'Maybe he went further afield, Scotland perhaps? Imagine living in Scotland?'

'Hard to get an approved travel permit out of Blissfordshire. He didn't have a high enough citizen score to own a car. If he'd gotten hold of an E-Wob Machina they would have traced that.'

Harry had a feeling they were keeping something back. He remembered how Stinker Rogers, Head of the Archaeology Department, who'd spent years digging up bits of Trollop Town, had dropped out of the news. His work had caused a stir both on the campus and off the campus. Stinker had overseen the 'Camelot Dig'. He claimed in front of an international media that if they could find Richard III under a carpark in Leicester there was no reason why the body of King Arthur shouldn't be under the Co-op in Trollop Town. The university milked it. Sir 'Gawain' Pinkerton was the VC at the time and the Bishop arranged several symposia exploring the link between Camelot and the university. That was before she'd gotten into aubergines. The university shot thirty places up the league table. There was talk of giving Rogers a Chair—the Arthurian Chair—with an accompanying round table and a Japanese toilet to boot. You only needed to give the command on your g-phone and your bottom would be cleansed by Cherry Blossom.

'That's right,' said Tristan. 'Larry Lomax goes back a long way. The university had recently taken on Professor Leech. It was Larry's first post I think. He was in his mid-twenties, a lecturer in theology. He was keen and upright. He told the *Chronicle* the Pro-Vice-Chancellor had been creaming off church funds into an offshore account. She risked being de-robed. Even the Bishop of Canterbury got involved.'

Leech had Larry's citizen score downgraded. He was made homeless and he had to move in with Fred Clueless. He was forced to learn Dewey Decimal Classification numbers off by heart which more or less broke him.

Then the recantation. Dr Lomax was hauled into the Board Room and made to read out a statement. He'd acted maliciously thanks to a theological disagreement on the question of forgiveness at the Croydon International Conference. The Pro-Vice-Chancellor had exposed, on his part, an over reliance on St Thomas Aquinas. He'd felt belittled but now he understood he should have seen this as part of the learning process.

'I can't for the life of me explain why I was overtaken by the desire to spread falsehoods about the Bishop. I give my heartfelt apologies for having besmirched her good name.'

The university had responded with understanding. The Department of Theology had offered him a post at the University of Rangoon which was now the University of Yangon.

The following day there was a procession in Trollop Cathedral. Imelda Wellbeloved was flanked by the Bishops of Trollop and Canterbury and she was praised for her integrity, theological rigour, and the act of forgiveness on her part which not only prevented Dr Lomax from undergoing criminal proceedings for defamation but which also allowed him to develop his career at a much respected Centre of Buddhist Studies.

Larry Lomax himself clad in a purple robe for the occasion came to the pulpit and uttered a very public Mia Culpa. He went on to read the beatitudes: Blessed are they who hunger and thirst for righteousness, for they shall be satisfied . . .

Days later there was a picture of a smiling Larry Lomax on the university portal, holding a passport, with the following statement: 'I'm thrilled to be furthering my career at the Centre of Buddhist Studies in Yangon. I shall be writing a book on Peace and Reconciliation dedicated to my mentor Professor Bishop Imelda Wellbeloved PHD.'

Months later the portal showed an out of focus picture of Larry outside the Shwedagon Pagoda and that was that. He drifted away. His book never saw the light of day. Some wondered whether he'd become a monk. Fare thee well Dr Lomax. Many thought him lucky to have escaped the university.

'What's this got to do with Stinker Rogers?' Harry asked.

'You never heard the rumours? The university shut down any discussion about Dr Rogers and all doomail correspondence about the Camelot dig vanished,' Tristan said.

'I mean the Camelot Dig,' Harry said. 'Stinker didn't find the body of King Arthur, we know that. I guess the whole thing was too much of an embarrassment given the media coverage. He'd let the university down and they got rid of him. They sacked him. They moved him on, made him an hourly paid Study Buddy at the University of Poke. I seem to remember the university slid fifty places down the league table.'

'It was worse than that,' Suki said. 'When Stinker sent off Arthur's bones for carbon dating they discovered they were the remains of Larry Lomax. Poor kid, he never did get the chance of pursuing his interest in Buddhist Studies, or anything else for that matter. He never made it out of Trollop Town. The Camelot dig became a crime scene.'

Tristan rolled a joint. Harry felt queasy. He went outside to get some air. The countryside looked eerily beautiful. A wild pony dawdled near a tree and a strange bird aeroplaned its way into the distance.

He went back into the house. Tristan was reading Gramsci. Suki was doing a head stand in the corner, her Korean feet pointing towards the ceiling.

'Go with Tristan to the shed. Be strong Harry. Be like tumbleweed.'

Chapter Eleven

———————

HEY OPENED the back gate, walked a while in silence, crossed the brook and watched the deer who were watching them. Tristan was humming Beethoven's 'Speaking Unto Nations' and he passed over the joint. It was beginning to drizzle. Harry was thinking of 'The Crucible of Change': 'Oh Nirvana, so glad are we you're not at the University of Botswana.'

The shed was damp. Tristan flicked a couple of switches.

'The quality isn't very good. We've watched it several times and we're working on the amplification and the visuals. I'm going to have to keep playing around with it. It's an old film. We managed to retrieve it from the Bishop's Wob Server.'

He started cranking the wheel and green data flicked across the screen.

'Get closer to the speakers.'

There was only static at first but soon enough there was chanting, the sound of a drum and then a church steeple came into view, lit by the moon.

'It jumps about.' Tristan was cranking the wheel and now there was a different light, indistinguishable voices and a walk-in freezer. In the freezer Harry could see a corpse hanging from a meat hook.

'Fuck Almighty!'

'It's the Peace and Reconciliation Centre, the other side of the graveyard. You know where I mean? Tristan asked.

'I wouldn't have thought the building was big enough to have a walk-in freezer.'

Tristan continued, 'It is. I've been there.'

'Me too,' said Harry, at least I've been to the reception. There were Buddhas everywhere and a print on the wall which had something to do with the Kabbala and if I remember rightly there was some information about a Toilet Twinning Campaign with the University of Khartoum.'

Tristan said, 'Last year Imelda called me in to do some copy editing for a Peace Conference in Shit Town. Some kind of outreach programme. As if all the peace and reconciliation in the world could reconcile the people of Shit Town to their shitty existence. I planted some auditory-visual spores around the building and when no one was around I went for a little walk. Bigger than you think. There's a corridor behind the reception area and at the end of the corridor there's a door which leads down to a basement. That's where the freezer is.'

'Are there any more bodies in the Centre of Peace and Reconciliation?'

'Who knows? This is an old film. There were boxes of aubergines everywhere. I didn't want to hang around in case the door closed and I got locked in. Keep watching. I'm going to crank up again.'

Harry could make out some of the people in the film, including the Bishop. The visuals stopped leaping about and Harry had a good look at the body laid out on the slab. Apart from a loin cloth the body was naked. He could see it was Stinker Rogers. Poor bastard. He thought he'd found the bones of King Arthur and now *he* was the exhibit.

There were several hooded figures. The Bishop was praying aloud: Abraham, Isaac. the Light of Idaho. A leather bag was placed on the table next to the body and a gloved hand picked out a collection of surgical knives and laid them out one by one.

Tristan tapped Harry on the shoulder: 'Things are going to get nasty.'

A hooded man sliced through the torso of Rogers and blood was everywhere. *The blood jet is poetry, there's no stopping it!* And then as if he were handing a newborn baby to its mother the 'doctor' was offering up Stinker's heart to the Bishop who wrapped it in cloth and out of the medical bag came a couple of axes.

'Did anyone remember to bring an electric saw?

The screen flickered, froze and popped. Harry stepped outside and vomited on some daffodils. After a couple of minutes Tristan appeared.

'Have you had enough?'

'I'm going for a walk.'

Dr Blink blinked and made use of the tissue Tristan had given him. There was some puke on his trousers. It was cold. He wasn't going to walk far and he had no idea of the direction he was going to take. He took out a cigarette—cheap fags from the Kurdish store. Risky. The police no doubt would have footage of these clandestine visits to the nondescript shop, a shop with only bottles of bleach and stale crisps on its shelves. Maybe the Kurd worked for the police? Harry could have his citizen score downgraded at any time. As if reading his thoughts the boy told him he could acquire illegal cigarettes in Shit Town too, though obviously these would be of a particularly shitty quality. Anyway, the Kurd continued, he shouldn't worry too much about it. Shit Town got a bad rap sometimes. There'd been rumours it was going to apply for city status.

Once it became Shit City it could put in a bid for the City of Culture 2040.

Harry bought Putin Plush at the Kurdish store. They tasted like Stalingrad but he had got used to it. It was an acquired taste, and right now Harry could do with the taste of Stalingrad to distract him from the film he'd been watching. They'd done away with Larry Lomax because he knew about the Bishop's financial dealings and they did away with Stinker Rogers because he discovered what they'd done to Larry. The university must have closed down the police enquiry. Convenient that the Chief Constable was one of the governors. To murder someone but then to cut out their heart and dismember them in some foul satanic ritual! Harry had to crouch behind a tree to get the flame from his lighter. His hands were shaking. A squirrel scrambled up the trunk. Harry had left his coat in the shed. He walked on anyway, all of a sudden wondering about the boy he hadn't seen for twenty years. Jacob would be twenty-five now or twenty-six. Concentrate. He hoped Jacob wasn't in Shit Town, or North Town, or anywhere in England for that matter.

He'd heard his ex-wife had gone to Uruguay and if he knew the boy were safe he would be happy enough. Jacob might have studied at university too. If it were a choice between the University of Montevideo or the University of Bliss it was a no brainer.

And if he were to see his son again and if his son were to ask 'How did you fight back against the spreadsheets, the sociopaths, the dwarves of thought, the infantilists, the corporate fixers, the mind blockers, the dog therapists, the brainless bureaucrats, the soul-shrinkers?' what would he say? I wrote a few disgruntled poems. I bought cut price cigarettes from a Kurdish kid. I wore my lanyard with reluctance.

Hannah Arendt said there wasn't much point being an inner émigré if the regime you despise continues to do as it wishes.

He lit another Stalingrad fag for the pleasure of the rust in his mouth and realised he'd walked further than he'd intended. The light was beginning to fade. He'd better make his way back to the shed. It was warmed by some kind of 1970s electric heater. He needed warmth. He took another drag and walked with resolution in the wrong direction.

The light was becoming white. Cloud cover, bird squawk. There was a gathering of deer, females, young males. They watched him carefully and they stood perfectly still as he walked towards them. He knew if they were real they would take flight at the last minute, running in all directions, curiosity turning into panic. And if they didn't run? He was close now. Harry could see them clearly, mute sirens drawing him in. He could almost touch them. He put out his hand and they fled.

He heard the sound in the sky, it was like a wound. He ducked down next to the trunk of an ash tree as the helicopter flew over. He watched it throwing its lights around. Military manoeuvres? The Compliancy Police? Harry's head began to spin. He waited for the helicopter to move away and waited a while to see if it would double back. He was almost certain he'd seen the letters UOB on the side of the helicopter. Perhaps the helicopter was being flown by Gladys Nirvana and her co-pilot was none other than the salivating Dean.

Oh Dean I think you're obscene. Oh Vice-Chancellor Nirvana, you'll never be the Dalai Lama.

He ought to be getting back. He felt like the loneliest monk.

It took a while to find the path back to the house. He heard the helicopter again but it was in the distance now. He could just about make out the shed and that was when he heard the dog.

'That's enough Jasper!'

Harry hid behind a bush and watched a man with an eye patch calling a Labrador to heel. The man took a biscuit out of his pocket.

'Sit, sit. Good dog, good dog.' The dog was drooling.

'Jasper, heel!' The man with the eye patch whistled and walked towards the shed. The dog started barking again. 'Enough Jasper, enough!' The dog's owner stood outside the shed. He took a phone out of his pocket and Harry strained to hear what he was saying. He wondered whether he'd been sent to kill Tristan. If the man with the eye patch had a gun should he try and tackle him? He could only presume that Tristan was in the shed lying low. Perhaps Tristan had a gun too? In fact he was certain he did. Suki would know how to get one. He had a feeling he was about to witness a shootout. The man put the dog on its lead and walked away.

Harry waited and watched. He walked around the shed and peered through the window. It was empty. The shed door was closed with the latch. Tristan must have gone back to the house. Harry needed to get back too; he needed to warm up. He needed to talk to Tristan and Suki.

It was getting dark now, still weeks before they changed the clocks. He had expected to see the house lit up, a log fire burning in the hearth but the house was lifeless. Harry walked cautiously towards the front door, squeezing out some light from his phone. He pushed against it. It was locked.

He knew the protocol. They had rehearsed these scenarios in the past. He made his way to what Tristan called Shed PB. He got in, wedged a chair against the door, and sat on the floor. His teeth were chattering.

CHAPTER TWELVE

Have you been to Havant?
No, I haven't.

ALL THE PRETZEL PROMISES in the world couldn't brighten the misery of the Bliss Train as it pulled out of Brackenhurst at six thirty Monday morning. Tristan and Harry weren't sitting next to each other, and further down in the cleaners' carriage there was Suki. Her hair was set in a bun. She was wearing her Bliss Cleaner's uniform, with its purple colours and stitched on logo—I Clean for Bliss, I Clean for the Light of Idaho.

Silas Squid was Cleaner in Chief, the El Supremo of the hoover. He'd worked at the university for thirty years and played a key role in helping the institution win The Glimmeringly Bright University Award. The university had won the award on eleven occasions. Twice it was runner up, pipped at the post.

Shine. Shine. Anodyne is the New Paradigm.

For Squid the Runner Up classification was a catastrophe. He cleaned with such zeal the staff wondered if his arms would fall off. The university had recognised his contribution by giving him a one percent pay rise, exceptional for university employees, unless they were Senior Management where large pay awards were handed out like vegetable samosas.

They had given Squid a one up, one down, grace and favour house in the Student Village—known as Squid House. He ran the Cleaning Team as if he were the head coach of England's rugby squad. Years of handling the Bliss Hoover Device had changed him. It would appear he had more than two arms and his eyes were strangely mismatched in the manner of a cephalopod and he had an uncanny ability to get himself into corners no regular human would be able to get into.

On one occasion Harry had called for a lift in the Boris Johnson Building. When the door slid open he thought some weary cleaner had left their hoover behind, exhausted after a twelve hour shift. When he looked again he realised Squid had assumed the horizontal position. The Cleaner in Chief rested on the surface of the floor. His limbs and tubes in balletic pose, a form of cephalopod mindfulness.

Many suspected Squid had intimate relations with the hoover, like alfalfa snout beetles who reproduce themselves. The Vice-Chancellor was mesmerized. She invited him over for tea. Squid zipped round her office, making strange noises. The force of his tube was so strong one of her Berlusconi-Gucci ankle boots was sucked right off.

She didn't know much about cephalopods but she'd love to experiment. When she had the Entomology Department up and running she might be able to get some funding for a mutation project. She could get back to that five-star general, friend of the president, if he hadn't been incarcerated in some lunatic asylum. Both cephalopods and hexapods had an impressive work ethic and being a scientist Nirvana was always keen to see how her employees might learn from the world beyond the classroom. It would be fun to drop Squid into a pot of boiling water to see what happened.

Nirvana made Squid into a university Spin–Off. His services contracted out (Bliss Squid Ltd.) He could manage a sixty-hour week without running to the union. The university gave him the new Hoover-Chattanooga Model at a special cleaning ceremony and put his face on the portal and threw in a twenty-pound hat voucher for the next Creativity and Play Festival. He was as happy as Larry. Academics should take note. They were always whining about workloads. New plans for a seven-day teaching week were now going through SMT -SIX-PAC.

Squid was irascible and had several run-ins with the Bishop concerning the generous depositions of Ethelred the Shitter. He was cavalier with his suction pads. No one had entered Squid House since that time the Dean of Divinity paid him a pastoral visit. The Dean never talked about it but thereafter he was a changed man. There was talk of his leaving the church altogether but Imelda lent him a copy of Julian of Norwich's *Divine Revelations* and allowed him to speak with the Light of Idaho on the Divinity Phone. He recovered his equilibrium and became the Bishop's most loyal lieutenant. Nevertheless there was always something peculiar about his eyes. There was always something peculiar about his theology.

Squid spawned. Two more cephalopod cleaners joined the Team. One had feminine features—Shelly. The other was gender fluid and they were called Shee.

Shee cleaned the Gender-Neutral lavatories with glee. When Harry and Tristan had their lavatorial trysts they had to be careful some long tube didn't wend its way into their booths. Roxana Grogan, on the other hand, rather liked it. As Head of the Office of Continuous Improvement she could relax. She enjoyed a warm feeling not only generated by her latest Bucharest toy but also charged with a professional glow which came from the knowledge her tenure had overseen the steady eradication of germs across the campus, the winning of several Glimmeringly Bright University Awards and a

Gold Medal for Upstanding Hygiene Zeal during the Gorilla Pox outbreak of 2030.

Squid's mismatched eyes provided an extensive field of vision and his movement across the campus was stealth like.

'Not wearing our lanyards today?' Or, 'This is a non-smoking campus Dr Blink'. (Harry was at the far end of the university, hiding ineffectively behind a bush.) 'I think the Management will take a dim view . . .'

Smokers, a recalcitrant group of self-immolators, were required to puff away in the Smoking Zone, known by Senior Management as BAD—Biological Antithetical Dynamics. It was a twentieth century prefab ready to go up in flames, which might well have been the Management's plan given their constant desire to cut posts. It was not a salutary experience standing in that reek of smoke yet it was an opportunity to touch base with fellow sufferers, many overweight, clearly not attending African Drumming Classes or Staff Badminton with any regularity. In that great smog messages were delivered by hand or mouth and the sharing of a new anecdote about the Dean of Discipline, or the VC, or the Bishop and there was always something new to say about Ethelred the Shitter.

Tristan had disabled the camera and the Smoking Zone—BAD— was beyond the remit of the Cleaning Team. The university had cooked up a deal with Trollop Council. It avoided university inspectors by technically being off campus.

There was a pleasure in making one's way to the Smoking Zone perched on the edge of the graveyard. It was an act of solidarity, *nostalgia de la boue*, a nod to Thanatos. Yet on a bright spring day Doctors Black, Blink and Lacan, game as a bagel after his unexpected professorial appointment, enjoyed a cigarette *en plein air*. Humph attached the word ELM to a Magnolia tree. He wanted to see if the Magnolia tree had some kind of ontological crisis.

Squid made monthly visits to the Dean's office, his notebook full of cephalopodic notes and names, and numbers and times and observations, the content of which he delivered in an unctuous Dickensian voice, 'Dean, there are several things which may be of interest . . .'

Squid was impressed by Professor Leech's metronomic toy, easy to clean when it was at rest. What did he think of the parrot? A shitloader with no respect for hierarchy, the Dean's bitch-parrot, a Rabelaisian splatterer of malevolent matter, a loose cannon? A skanky enigma? He couldn't help licking his lips as he left the office. When the moment came he would attach a tube with a wide circumference and suck the parrot straight into the Hoover's bowels.

Squid had an Achilles heel. The proximity of Squid House to student accommodation meant he found his way into student bedrooms. Tentacles roamed freely. Female students found their underwear had disappeared. Boys complained trainers had gone too, either the left foot, or the right, hardly ever an entire pair—not to mention essay notes, unused condoms, stashes of Charlie. Izzy, one of Harry's students, complained she'd woken in the early hours to find Squid under her bed.

Harry received a poem on his doomail called 'Night Fever': 'You took me in your arms / then I realised you had more arms than the average man / Oh no, oh no . . .'

Tristan filmed Squid floating down the corridor of a student house at four in the morning, his tubes and suction pads lighting up like a Neapolitan firework display.

Tristan had enough on Squid to make his tentacles shrink. The university paid him very little, notwithstanding the one percent pay rise. Squid was excited when extra pounds came his way. He spent the money on cleaning agents. There was a particularly efficacious one manufactured on the outskirts of Chernobyl. Other than a subscription to *Germ Free Quarterly* Squid had few interests. One year he went on a package holiday to Portugal.

Tristan had enough stuff on the cephalopod. He wondered whether they could turn Squid completely, make him an informer. He would have a lot to say. Tristan slipped him fresh mackerel and cuttlefish. Squid was moved to tears, rivers of tears.

Suki put her sunglasses on and a recycled Pandemic mask. She was mindful of facial recognition cameras and she knew she couldn't hang around. She had little more than ten minutes to place high-viz-high-volume auditory spores in the Dean's office and open the back door of his Super Wob. She'd pieced together, with the help of Tristan and Squid, a breakdown of his movements. From ten in the morning he would be in crisis meetings with Senior Management and they had an important agenda—A Cost Cutting Project: Can We Get Rid of Fifty Academics without causing the usual fuss? The meeting started at ten but there was always the chance Leech could swing back to his office. Bishop Wellbeloved would be in that meeting too. However at eleven the Dean of Divinity would be paying her a visit. He had written a hermeneutic study of seminal aubergines in the Old Testament.

The office of VC Nirvana was unbreachable. Her PA—Ms Celia Midnight—would be at her desk the entire morning. The VC's PA would be expecting Shelley. Nothing to be done.

Thanks to Squid, Suki had a Cleaner's Touch Card which let her into the Dean's office. Suki pulled down the Venetian blinds and disabled the surveillance camera. She took out her duster and charged up the Chattanooga Hoover and studied the lay out of the office. She had to work quickly. Events in the Forest had queered the pitch.

The metronomic toy was resting. The parrot in sleep mode. She sat at the Dean's Wob Top Super X. It didn't take her long to break in. The Dean had been a little lax with his Wob Top Pass Code, spending too much time listening to *Je t'aime* and massaging Nirvana's feet. She got in far enough to leave auditory spores and conceal evidence of her tampering. Her heart was beating fast. She had not done this for a long time but it felt good, with her I Clean for Bliss, I Clean for the Light of Idaho stitched onto her cleaner's uniform.

'Ten Minutes! Ten fucking minutes!' the parrot screamed. Suki dropped her USB and shouted an expletive in Korean. She had no more than two minutes to finish up, cover her tracks. Her heart was racing now. As she slipped out of the office green gruel splattered her left shoulder.

'I am not Flaubert's parrot, I am not the Dean's parrot, I'm a big fucking nasty Nigerian parrot!'

She walked through the Crimson Building, past Leech, and made her way to the Gender-Neutral lavatories. They'd been up all night running through the plans but they hadn't given any thought to the parrot. She twisted herself around to see the shit on her shoulder and she stepped into a booth to get some high-quality paper. She dabbed a fistful of it in water and set about cleaning herself. Awkward.

The door opened. Mr Nobody was wearing fishnet stockings and there was a dab of rouge on his cheeks. He was carrying a black canvas bag. He smiled and said 'Morning duck' and made his way into a booth. On the door was a poster which said Compassion for the Self and Compassion for Others. On the next door there was a poster which said Toilet Paper Needs Us Too.

Too late to change plans. She heard Nobody tapping the flush button before breaking into 'I've put a spell on you . . .' Suki padded down the corridor before emerging into the Plaza and a magnolia tree under which a group of giggling Japanese students was taking selfies.

She stood outside the Bishop's office in the Fairly Old Building and cleared her head. At least the Pro-Vice chancellor didn't have a shit-squirting parrot. She tapped her Bliss Card and she was in. She remembered from a visit many years ago—an invitation to discuss Shintoism—the great episcopal throne. On the wall there was a painting of Julian of Norwich, which had a passing resemblance to Imelda herself, under which emblazoned in the colour purple: 'All shall be well, and all manner of things shall be well.'

Above the Bishop's desk was a map of Idaho. The room smelt of lavender and cannabis oil and something a little sweet and sour, like a vase of flowers on the way out. She disabled the surveillance camera. It was harder to get into the Bishop's Wob Top Super X Idaho model. The old girl clearly knew something about Wob Top security. Suki had to work quickly, concentrate, focus. She glanced at the clock on the wall—fifteen minutes before the Dean of Divinity swung round for their meeting on hermeneutic aubergines.

The silence was broken by a Gregorian chant. Suki hit the wrong key and the screen slid away. Shit! The chanting came from a thin vertical Art Deco phone piece. The room was taken over by monks' voices. Suki jabbed the keyboard to retrieve the Blake Resistance Pathway. Did the chanting mean the lady bishop was about to appear? The chanting stopped and she heard a soft American drawl drifting out of the handset:

'Imelda dear, I am *so* sorry to have missed you. I guess you're busy in the service of the Light of Idaho. I have great news about the PL1—the Peerless Lachrymose One—Peace be upon him, her, they, peace be upon everyone. I've made a decision about lending the miracle to the University of Bliss. Speak to you later alligator. In a while croque monsieur.'

It was ten-fifty. Tick Tock. In the far corner of the Bishop's room the growling began and the Shih Tzu attached its teeth to the left ankle of the intruder. Suki managed not to shout out. She used her free leg to hoist the dog into the air and administer a couple of karate chops. She dropped the Shih Tzu into the wastepaper basket. The dog tuned green, then red, its paws rigid, facing upwards, bleeping. Suki spent thirty seconds signing out of the Bishop's Wob Top in a non-detectable mode. She gathered up the hoover and limped out of the room.

From one side of the corridor walked the Dean of Divinity, eyes ablaze; from the other the Pro-Vice-Chancellor.

'Morning, morning, blissful mornings, lachrymose mornings! Ha! Ha! Ha!'

They nodded at the cleaner. Suki got out of the building and checked her ankle. There was a trail of blood in the Fairly Old Building.

CHAPTER THIRTEEN

D R BLINK had hunkered down in the Percy Bysshe shed for a couple of hours, hardly daring to move. He listened out for dog noises and at some point he heard barking in the distance. Tristan turned up at last and they slipped into the house, lit candles, drew the curtains. They threw a rug at Harry and told him to stoke the fire and drink whisky. Suki and Tristan spoke in low animated voices. Harry fell asleep. Only to be awakened early. It was already time to catch the train.

Monday morning. He wasn't feeling chipper as he stepped into Wow Wow Room 17 for his eight o'clock Pop-Up Poetry class.

'Morning class.' Dr Blink didn't expect a reply.

A couple of students had their heads down on their tables, the rest were tapping their g-phones. The girl with the learning contract sat under her desk wearing rabbit ears which lit up when she shook her head. Only Magda said 'Morning Dr Blink'.

'The poem for discussion,' Blink said with an attempt at enthusiasm given his lack of sleep, 'is called 'I am the last' which is a prose poem by Charles Simic.'

Maurice said, 'Didn't Emily Dickinson get trapped in prose?'

'You're right,' said Harry. He found himself quoting the verse:

> They shut me up in Prose—
> As when a little Girl
> They put me in the Closet—

'Ouch,' whispered Milly, 'trapped in prose, doesn't sound good.'

'Trapped in poetry would be worse,' said Zac.

'What would she have said about being trapped in a prose poem?'

'I guess we'll never know, Maurice.'

The kid looked pleased with himself. He seemed taller. Cleverness was a growth hormone.

Molly said, 'My mother says she feels trapped in her job.'

Harry hoped he'd never have to meet Molly's mother.

Tulip, aka Jackson, said, 'You know, this is relatable.'

Dan said, 'I literally saw a book called *Taking off Emily Dickinson's Clothes*.'

Laughter. The class was waking up, or at least some of the class was waking up. Harry needed more coffee.

'Typical,' Izzy said, 'it must have been written by some creepy old man.'

'It's a book of poems,' Harry said, surprised one of his students had come across it. Surprised the book hadn't been pulped. Who knows what had happened to the author? Harry had met him in the twentieth century. They'd stood side by side in a urinal on the east coast of England and cracked jokes about literary festivals. They were at a literary festival. They didn't have literary festivals anymore. They had social media events where they promoted *Pure Reflectivity* and pulled Mary Beard out of her care home to make some intelligent observations about the Romans which no one could understand.

'How can you call a book *Taking off Emily Dickinson's Clothes*?' Laura asked.

'I reckon you can call a book anything you want,' Harry said. Careful. Careful.

'Did you know Emily Dickinson?' someone asked.

Someone piped up 'Taking off Gladys Nirvana's Clothes. The Vice-Chancellor's Strip Tease. I do it exceptionally well. I do it so it feels like heaven and then I do it so it feels like hell . . .'

Harry smiled to himself and realised the kid's joke might help him. He had long suspected the Vice-Chancellor enjoyed taking off her clothes. In fact, the word 'alacrity' came to mind.

He thought about Roxana Grogan with a butt plug up her Ass of Continuous Improvement. Harry blocked out the thought. It wasn't even nine o'clock.

'Shall we get back to the poem?' he said.

They opened their Just Touch Me Reading Packs and Harry clicked open the Wob Screen.

'Have you found it? Good. I'm going to read it out and then we'll see if anyone would like to make some observations.'

'Can I read it?' said Magda.

'Go for it!'

I am the last Napoleonic soldier. It's almost two hundred years later and I am still retreating from Moscow. The road is lined with white birch trees and the mud comes up to my knees. The one-eyed woman wants to sell me a chicken, and I don't even have any clothes on.

The Germans are going one way; I am going the other. The Russians are going still another way and waving good-by. I have a ceremonial saber. I use it to cut my hair, which is four feet long.

Jack said 'It's shorter than *War and Peace*.'

'Have you read *War and Peace*?' Maurice asked.

'I read the first two pages.'

'That's probably enough,' continued Maurice. 'This piece by Simic is a summary of *War and Peace* with a futuristic add on.'

Beth said without malice: 'You're such a clever bastard Maurice.'

Izzy said, 'I'm no military historian but I would have thought being in Russia without clothes wouldn't have helped.'

'You're not supposed to take it literally,' Emily said.

'I have an image of a naked Frenchman in my head.'

'Oh là là!'

'All that snow, *brrr* so cold; he would have been a little shrivelled in the artillery department,' Frankie said.

Magda said, 'My family has told me stories about World War Two. Poland suffered much—Germans and Russians invaded our country. People were killed in the thousands. Jews were taken to Auschwitz. Gypsies were killed. People had nothing to eat—a chicken would have been a luxury.'

There was silence and Harry wondered whether Magda would continue. After a while she did: 'If you live under a dictatorship you're not free to say what you think. You have to be careful about everything. You're always being watched. Even writing a poem could be dangerous. Osip Mandelstam wrote 'The Stalin Epigram'. Stalin was angry the poet had written about the cockroaches above his lips. Mandelstam died on the way to a gulag. Poems are dangerous because they are true. This poem by Simic makes me sad. I like it. It has atmosphere. It is short and it is beautiful.'

Maurice asked 'Do you think the poem is examining Nietzsche's concept of Eternal Recurrence?'

Beth asked whether the ceremonial sabre was a phallic symbol.

Tulip Jackson said, 'I am sick to death of phallic symbols.' They stood up and left the room.

Let's Face the Music and Dance.

One of his students had written another poem called 'Screaming into the Void'.

> I scream into the Void
> like a paranoid android.
>
> I have
> fallen into
> an existential cavity
>
> where there's very little gravity.
> An ontological hole
>
> like an Abbess in the Abyss
> like a mole.
>
> I scream at oblivion
> like an outraged Bolivian
>
> *hoping and hoping*
> > *something*
> > > *bounces back . . .*

Good luck with that Chloe.

At eleven o'clock there was a fifteen-minute break. Harry shoved a handful of Pro Plus pills into his mouth and thought about the poem he was supposed to be writing for the Vice-Chancellor's inaugural lecture.

He wrote:

THE UNIVERSITY OF BLISS BELIEVES IN DEVELOPING THE INDIVIDUAL IN A GLOBAL CONTEXT—WE BELIEVE IN CHALLENGING THE STATUS QUO. WE ARE A HEDGEHOG FRIENDLY CAMPUS.

He wrote:

~~I am an ocean-soaked immigrant. I want to be a participant.~~

~~I'm on benefits. I'm a lesbian Muslim who suffers from OCD.~~
~~What can the university do for me?~~

~~I am a Pagan, Polyamorous Post-Apartheid Priest. I am unleavened~~
~~bread.~~
~~I am yeast. I am a moveable feast.~~

~~I am a Transgender Syrian refugee. I shot Omar El Sharif (a vegan).~~
~~I did not shoot the deputy.~~

~~I am a vegetarian cross-dressing atheist. I have tried most things—~~
~~I have not yet tried being a Satanist.~~

Rather quickly he put several lines through it. He wondered whether the surveillance camera had photographed his notes.

Then out of nowhere he had a memory of Venice. This was before the change. Before the National Alliance Party had come to power. He would never go to Venice again but in his head he was walking along its canals and walking across its bridges. For a moment he felt sheer joy then he felt as if someone had kicked him in the stomach. He wrote 'The Academic Bridge of Sighs':

> The lagoon police are underneath
> the Bridge of Sighs,
>
> another death by hanging,
> another academic dies.
>
> That last email from the Dean
> broke the camel's back.
>
> The wretched man was stretched
> and stretched upon the rack.

Chapter Fourteen

D
R BLINK blinked. He was awake. Sunday morning, the bed
upstairs was rocking. He'd missed the foreplay. Norbert
had gotten to the top of his Carpathian Mountain and
Natasha had become the leading soprano in some dissonant opera,
something by Berg perhaps.

The storm abated. The ceiling was intact. Norbert's heavy
tread down the Victorian stairs shook the building. The front door
slammed and the man with the pork pie gene slouched off to 'Tran-
sylvania', the eatery around the corner. There were schnitzels to
prepare and bowls of gloop. And Transylvanian Crystal to sell to a
beleaguered queue of South Town addicts.

Harry dragged himself out of bed—almost paid for now. He
needed coffee. Not easy to get decent coffee in South Town. There'd
been another spike in the price. He knew an Albanian who could get
something 'Italian style' in a big colourless tin.

One could only imagine what it was like in Shit Town. It'd been
a long week—teaching, grading, doomails, forms to fill out, online
compliancy courses, the creation of learning outcomes, the writing
of trigger warnings and lots of other university shit.

Tristan had said there needed to be minimum contact. Or perhaps better still no contact. The Dean was in Panopticon Mode. The

behaviour of lecturers in the Department of 'Creative Shite-ing' would be noted with interest from this point on. There was a need for vigilance. There was a need to monitor the fallout from that weird Sunday and the subsequent undercover work on the part of Suki. The Dean went berserk when he discovered parrot shit on his office door and the Bishop had a spiritual crisis when she found Ethelred in the waste paper basket. His little paws were sticking out in supplication, flashing out the colours of the rainbow in dysfunctional techno mode.

Tristan and Suki paused the Blake Programme. They needed to see how much the university knew about their hacking operations, if indeed they knew anything at all.

Tristan put the shed into lockdown. He covered up the electronic paraphernalia with tarpaulin and attached a micro camera to the ceiling.

Harry's knight in armour was chortling. Harry sipped the coffee. It wasn't great; at least it was strong. If he had his cut-price Stalingrad cigarettes this was his Stalingrad coffee. He liked to imagine he was a scar-faced colonel in the Wehrmacht. There had been a lull in the campaign and the colonel was in a field tent poring over maps of the broken city. He was smoking a Stalingrad cigarette. He was, after all, in Stalingrad and his batman had come in with a chipped mug of ersatz coffee—*Eine Tasse Kaffee Herr Oberst.* The battle-weary Colonel, an old-fashioned Prussian officer, looked at the young soldier and thought about his son, of similar age, whom he hadn't heard from for months. He had no idea whether he'd been taken prisoner or killed. 'Thank you soldier' and then the colonel said, as if they were passing in some quiet street in Berlin, 'How are you today Heinrich?'

The soldier found himself blushing—blushing in Stalingrad, he was still young enough to blush.

The coffee tasted like boots yet the illusion of *Eine Tasse Kaffee* was a gift, taking the colonel for a moment to that place with chandeliers and fine pastries along the Kurfürstendamm, thousands of miles from the carnage. He dismissed the soldier wondering how long it would be before the boy was snuffed out by a sniper or a bomb.

Doctors Blink and Black had found another way of communicating. Harry had chanced upon a red telephone box off the Mutant Mile, behind the Church of Emmanuel.

The South Town Council put a protection order on red telephone boxes. They sent an employee to track them down. This was followed by a debate in the townhall. What should they do with them? Outreach for the homeless? A phone box could be rented out for the night. The 'standing tenant' would have to sleep in the upright position, but at least they would be dry, and they could listen to a recording at no extra charge: how to write a job-grabbing CV.

The Red Telephone Box Project Manager invited VC Nirvana to make a motivational speech.

'Living in crimped conditions didn't stop Nelson Mandela from becoming the President of South Africa,' Gladys pronounced.

Imelda came along too. 'The phone box is like a coffin, a *momento mori*. The poor should never be afraid of death.'

The Minister for Rough Sleeping was driven down in a limousine and stood alongside the VC and her deputy for a photograph. When asked if he would like to sleep in a telephone box he said, 'No, I wouldn't. Absolutely not.'

Under cover of darkness old men pissed in the red telephone boxes with longing and nostalgia. Some attached personal ads: Pensioner seeks dominatrix, into leather and Lapsang Souchong.

Some lazy dappled day Harry stepped into the box. The urinous tang set off a memory. A sequence of numbers arranged itself in his head. He put an absentminded hand into a pocket of coins, inserted one into the slot and rang the number. The line crackled into life. Such a beautiful dialling tone. 'Hello,' the voice said, 'Annabelle speaking . . .'

He put another coin into the slot but the line cut out and he pulled out the coins from his pocket and saw to his surprise there were a couple of euros. The dialling tone started again and the voice said, 'Hello, hello, this is Annabelle speaking' and he put in another euro and said, 'Annabelle this is Harry, remember Harry?'

'No I'm afraid I don't.'

When he got home he opened drawers and cupboards and went through the lining of jackets looking for more euros, remnants of another age. He couldn't find any. It wasn't going to be easy to get hold of any new ones. Inhabitants of South Town were never going to get a European Travel Pass.

The Curry in A Hurry Mini Mart had bought out the Polish delicatessen. Europeans had been encouraged to repatriate. How did Norbert manage? Outside his shop Ahmed laid out his aubergines: the bulbous and the eel-like, boxes of jostling, living aubergines like fish in an Italian market, a patchwork of quivering purple.

Ahmed was astute. If you gave him ten pounds he'd hand you five Euros in return.

Harry popped the coins into his pocket and bought himself a medium-sized aubergine. He would eat it later, sliced and grilled. He would have to use Grade 2 vegetable oil. Olive oil was above his pay grade and in any case he needed a Good Behaviour Voucher to even think about buying some.

Walking along the Mutant Mile towards his lodgings Harry spotted the man with the eye patch. There was no sign of a dog. The man was near Harry's place and Harry couldn't tell whether he'd been seen or not but now the man—Harry decided to call him Colonel Crunch—was walking away.

When Harry got into his flat he saw that a large envelope had been pushed under the door. He put down the aubergine. He picked up the envelope and a handful of photographs fell on the floor. His hands were shaking.

Harry sat on the sofa and reached for his reading glasses. He put the photographs close to his face and squinted at them and then he pushed them away from himself to look from a distance. It seemed they had been taken at night. Difficult to see anything in some of the photographs. He could see there was a graveyard. Harry switched on a table lamp and flicked through the photographs again. The Bishop was wearing a hood and she appeared to be holding something in her hands. Flicking through the pictures Harry could make out Derek Nobody, Saffron Fraud, Roxana Grogan, the Lego Woman, Squid, the Dean of Divinity and a thin boy in spectacles who looked a lot like Maurice.

Humph was in the graveyard too. Some grave-switching game? I thought I'd died in 1870. Non non, it was 1789, Zut, zut . . . Had he crossed over to the other side? Had the bastard betrayed them? There were torches, unrecognisable icons, a flare light. There was someone clutching a crucifix. And one could see a name on a tombstone: Benjamin Tulip—or was it Hewlett? He'd died in 1915. A soldier? There was no sign of Gladys Nirvana or the Dean of Discipline.

Harry took some paracetamol, increasingly hard to come by these days, and drank the dregs of the Stalingrad coffee. He left the house with five euros in his pocket. He walked down the Mutant Mile, cut through the Rue des Merdes de Chiens and made his way towards the Church of Emmanuel, past the Zimbabwean goat butchers and he was overtaken by a legless man in a mobility buggy, blasting out 'Who Let the Dogs Out'. The phone box was plastered with cards: 'Into spanking and short walks, also partial to Ovaltine'.

He slid a coin into the slot and dialled.

'Am I speaking to Dr Black?'

'You'd better make it quick; there could be a trace on this.'

'I'm calling from a telephone box.'

'Quick is always good Dr Blink.'

'Photographs under my door . . .'

The line made a beeping noise and Harry put in another euro.

'People in a graveyard . . .'

'Somewhere safe.'

The line became crackly again and words were chewed up.

'What do you mean eye patch?'

'That man with the eye patch.'

'Did you notice which eye was patched over?'

The last euro slid hungrily into the slot.

CHAPTER FIFTEEN

'In April, the month when purple arums reared their hoods in the yam-
fields, there were fresh rumours . . .'

—*The Viceroy of Ouidah*, Bruce Chatwin

PROFESSOR IMELDA WELLBELOVED, the Pro-Vice-Chancellor, was chairing a Senior Management meeting under the auspices of SMT-SIX-PAC. There were several university governors in attendance and various businessmen, and a couple of lanyard-wearing businesswomen. The Academic Representative was the Head of Sports Studies. Chief Facilitator Ryan was wearing a track suit with the Team Bliss logo.

Imelda was received with a great deal of sympathy. Good coffee and pyramids of sandwiches were laid out on a table which had been graced with a white tablecloth. Everyone knew about the Bishop's existential crisis. This wasn't the first. Crisis was a sign of spiritual quest. Despair—the sin of Accidie—was the hallmark of a soul which had been tested on the bumpy road to redemption.

When she'd discovered Ethelred upside down in the wastepaper bin bleeping electronically in the colours of the rainbow she let out a theological whimper. She picked the dog up and held it to her heart. The little shitter wouldn't have got in the wastepaper bin and disabled itself voluntarily. It suggested the Shih Tzu had been attacked, wounded and thrown aside. Not only had Ethelred cost fifteen thousand pounds, but the Bishop had also developed a spiritual bond with that winsome creature. In her grief Professor Wellbeloved couldn't remember the details of the insurance policy regarding top of the range Tibetan Shih Tzus. Could Ethelred be sent to the Super Plus Repair Shop? Would she be able to get a replacement? If the university accountant wasn't forthcoming she could always turn to the Light of Idaho who believed all creatures were blessed whether they were made of flesh or whether they were vegetal or hexapodal. The Church of the Aubergine had nothing against dogs. The Platonic Dog was an anagram of the Platonic God. Among its congregation there were hyenas and goats of an unorthodox persuasion and wailing yams and ladies' fingers and dung beetles. These were Ignatius Loyola's latest foot soldiers. Gladys rather liked that.

When VC Nirvana heard about the Shih Tzu she gloated. She knew she shouldn't but gloating was such fun. Gladys understood the Light of Idaho was the money pump yet she couldn't rid herself of that irritation every time she saw her second-in-command waddle around the campus with that incontinent dog.

Gladys asked after it, even patted it, in a manner of speaking. However she could tell that ever since the cake incident the dog didn't like her. She didn't like the dog either. At a drinks party in the Senior Common Room she gave Ethelred a kick with her Berlusconi-Gucci boot, the one with the pointed toe. The dog yelped. Gladys pretended she'd stood on it by mistake.

'Oh what a careless Vice-Chancellor I am!'

Imelda gave her a peculiar look when she held the dog in her arms. If the dog could have talked at that moment it would have snitched willingly.

In her desperation the Bishop had even entertained the thought the office intruder had been sent by Nirvana. Had Squid done something with his Chattanooga Hoover? It appeared the camera in her office had malfunctioned that morning so there was no footage of anyone in her office. Even the dictatorial Dean crossed her mind. He seemed to be developing an unexpectedly close relationship with the VC and was prone to irascible outbursts.

The Bishop held the purple aubergine card, the money card. Who would dare to cross her? When Ethelred was undergoing a six-hour operation her mind drifted towards the 'Creative Shite-ing Department'. She couldn't rid herself of the VC's joke even though she disapproved of it. What about Drs Blink and Black? And could she be certain Prof Humph Lacan was on her side? He knew so much now. Had she been too soft on the writers and the artists? She loved poetry and enjoyed the Dean's irritation when she argued poetry had its place on the curriculum. Poetry cleansed her soul when it felt besmirched. Notwithstanding her kumquat mediation sessions her soul never enjoyed that spiritual quickening she longed for. Although she was but a phone call away from the Light of Idaho she was conscious of an unbearable weight.

The VC had sanctioned medical expenses. Imelda was loathe to go for the replacement package. The vet flew in with an assistant and they set up a field hospital in the Senior Common Room. The room was cordoned off for several days. Ethelred wasn't dead. The Shih Tzu, it appeared, was in a Shih Tzu coma, emanating occasional strangulated bleeps. It was a classic case of PTSD, Dr Kim said. The dog's brain to body functionality had to be re–digitized. Ethelred was wired up to a Shooter Poot. The assistant attached acupuncture needles to encourage blood flow. It was hard to persuade the Bishop to leave the room.

'I will give you my report as soon as I've finished,' Dr Kim said. 'It is clear Model 378 X has experienced a break down in the Axon neurological structure, owing to trauma administered by an unknown force.'

He wondered whether the assailant might have had some training in martial arts.

Ethelred recovered and the vet handed over a clinical report, as well as a large bill. This confirmed the Bishop's suspicions. The vet, with female assistant, flew back to Tibet—executive class. Ethelred made good progress. If anything his anal functionality was charged up even more. His IQ quota had been upgraded too. The Bishop fed the dog with chicken hearts. She dabbed her eyes and prayed. Mostly she dabbed her eyes.

For three days it had been touch and go. Dr Kim and his assistant slept in made up beds in the Senior Common Room. The assistant had brought a travel wok and a portable stove.

When the emergency had passed Dr Kim and his assistant took up rooms at an expensive hotel. During the day they ran intelligence, compliancy and cognitive tests at the university and a Level Two Programme was installed.

They put the dog on the table. 'Good morning Ethelred.'

'Good morning. Some days I am Ethelred, some days I am Ethel. We hope you enjoy your time at the University of Bliss.'

His little head moved winningly and it barked. *Woof. Woof.*

The Bishop held her arms in the air and opened her mouth. Dr Kim said, 'Excellent start. We will be able to install more sophisticated programmes remotely. They are very expensive.'

Imelda said, 'Don't worry about that.'

The meeting of Senior Management along with governors and wealthy stakeholders was scheduled to take place at eleven o'clock in the Board Room. Various members had sloped in early to eye up the spread and grab some coffee, ready to extend their best wishes to the Bishop, if they'd not already done so. VC Nirvana was holding a bouquet of flowers which she pressed into the arms of her deputy and pecked both cheeks if only to catch a whiff of cannabis.

Four weeks had passed since the Shih Tzu incident and having got over the gloating VC Nirvana said to herself, 'Gladys, the long game, focus on the long game.'

She was genuinely disturbed when she saw the crumpled Bishop. A week later she took Imelda out for a dinner. She got Terry to drive her to Trollop Town and take her back home later so she could make her way through some excellent post-Brexit wine. The University Gold Platinum Expenses card sat snugly in the lined pocket of her Berlusconi-Gucci handbag.

'And I'd like a foot massage when I get home!'

It was a while since he'd done the honours.

Having wept into her napkin the Bishop expressed relief Ethelred was on the mend. It was over the cheeseboard she laid out her embryonic plan for the staff cutting exercise. VC Nirvana cracked a joke about the Creative Shite-ing Department. The Bishop giggled liturgically and choked on a truffle.

'Have some more wine,' the Vice-Chancellor said.

By the time Senior Management arrived at the Board Room there was a fly buzzing around. Derek Nobody, wearing a suit, was explaining to a local entrepreneur that academics were a dying breed and ought to be put out of their misery. Or made into Pedagogical Bots or better still worked to death. Or all of the above. A campus without malodorous academics would be a much lovelier campus.

The businessman was saying, 'I suppose someone has to stand in front of the Wob Wob Board and move their arms around.'

'Pity we can't just find some arms and then we wouldn't have to worry about sick pay.'

'Why not cancel sick pay altogether?'

'We're working on that,' Derek Nobody said. 'We're also working on the seven-day non-weekend model of teaching. The union will whinge like hell but who gives a shit.'

'Beautiful.'

'This hogwash about zero-hour contracts. Academics ought to see the positives. Burger flippers get £11 per hour; and we pay our Staff Study Buddies with a PHD £14 an hour, that's three pounds more! And £12 if they haven't yet completed. We give them so much admin most of them never do!'

One of the businesswomen—who owned a chain of hotels and had a special lanyard bobbing round her neck—said 'My niece, at a loose end after finishing her doctorate dipped her toe into academia and found the £14 per hour didn't include the grading and admin duties, and that if you counted it all out the pay rate was about £5 per hour. She became an investment banker.'

'Clever girl!'

Derek Nobody laughed. 'Five pounds per hour is better than no pounds an hour. If teaching staff want to earn more they could take up a shelf stacking job at one of our new Global Britain supermarkets.'

'Exactly,' said Ms Grogan and she blushed. If she moved quickly she could feel the butt plug. The one she'd inserted that morning was rather large and it was connected to an electronic device controlled remotely by a BSDM master in Bucharest.

One of the governors, an American from Missoula, said 'These new CIA-sponsored post-Brexit burger joints are doing a great job. The beef is real tasty but full of compliancy hormones. The poor are getting fatter and more obedient by the day.'

'Let's drink to that!' said the Vice-Chancellor. 'Is there anything stronger than coffee?' she said to one the catering staff, a former student. The young man hurried across the graveyard to the Centre for Peace and Reconciliation and came back with several bottles of fizz.

Spring sunshine glinted off the governors' lanyards. It was less than a year since VC Nirvana's appointment. Notwithstanding Ethelred's misadventure there were reasons to be upbeat. University managers had received a bonus and the union was mostly well behaved. The dead hand of bureaucracy squashed any flicker of creativity and there were rumours the University of Bliss was climbing up the League Table. The Dean had set up a collaborative project with the Harbin Institute of Technology and he'd approached the Swiss town of Wankdorf. He'd also upgraded the university's surveillance system. Two members of staff had published peer reviewed articles promoting the virtues of *Pure Reflectivity*. Professor Peacock had scooped an award at the World Lego Convention.

Imelda was facing personal dog sorrow but she was dealing with it.

Gladys was saying 'I think the teaching staff are too keen to express a point of view. I'm all for points of view if they express my point of view.'

The Bishop asked the Dean of Divinity to help with the presentation. He hadn't given up on the Anglican liturgy altogether. He loved Evensong. Rituals made him tremble.

Professor Leech looked at the Vice-Chancellor's boots. His tongue moved across his lips.

VC Nirvana called the gathering to order. She announced the return of Bishop Wellbeloved. There was a round of applause.

'Thank you, thank you,' said the Bishop in her purple cloak, her lips twitching. She turned to the Dean of Divinity. 'Would you,

Marcus?' Her assistant took the bouquet from the Bishop's hands and left the room. Imelda was rather enjoying the delay. Soon they heard barking and in came the Dean of Divinity with Ethelred.

Another round of applause, much louder this time. Marcus took the lead off and the dog rushed up to the Bishop and licked her face.

'That will do,' the Bishop said and the dog calmed down.

The Dean of Divinity manoeuvred a small table to the front of the room and placed the dog in the middle of it.

'Sit Ethel, sit Ethelred,' said the Bishop. 'There's a good thing.'

The Bishop was feeling giddy. She could feel a small aubergine in one of her pockets. It might turn into a Baba Ghanoush if she got over-excited.

'Good morning Ethelred.'

'Good morning,' the dog replied. 'Some days I am Ethelred, some days I'm Ethel. We hope you enjoy your time at the University of Bliss.'

Its little head moved coyly and it barked. *Woof. Woof.*

There was an intake of breath.

Gladys said sotto voce 'The Bishop's good, fucking good.'

'Would you like to say a little more Ethelred?'

'I am obedient and punctual and believe in spiritual values and I believe in diversity. I believe in challenging the status quo and I believe in re-cycling. I welcome toilet-twinning projects with the University of Lagos. I believe in small animals like the hedgehog and the country mouse. The University of Bliss is a hedgehog friendly campus.'

Derek Nobody was getting an erection.

'I'm doing training courses in data protection and hybrid teaching and I am resilient. I believe in the student experience and emotional wellbeing and I believe in large salaries for Senior Management and their friends. I particularly value dog stroking, especially when I'm the strokee.'

Saffron Fraud dropped her g-phone and opened her mouth. The fly swooped.

'I believe in the governors, the Vice-Chancellor, the Pro-Vice-Chancellor and their loyal lieutenants. I believe in the Light of Idaho.'

I suppose that had to come into it, Gladys said to herself.

'Thank you, Ethelred, or should I say Ethel?' the Bishop said.

'I'm both Ethelred and Ethel. I am a non-binary Shih Tzu. I am the original non-binary Shih Tzu and I have a tree named after me. It's called the Shih Tzu tree.'

'Do you like poetry?'

'I am learning to write haikus. Small poems are like small dogs.'

Everyone laughed apart from Professor Leech.

'Would you like to recite a poem?'

The dog's ears lit up, digesting the instruction, and somewhat to the embarrassment of the Bishop, a blob of excrement shot across the room. There was a sound like a tape recorder in fast forward mode—words spitting out in in a squeaking spooling rush.

'Marcus, could you fine tune the programme?'

The Divinity Dean was crouched over a portable Wob.

The dog growled, re-positioned itself. Somewhat robotically it chanted:

> The woods are lovely, dark and deep,
> But I have promises to keep,
> And miles to go before I sleep,
> And miles to go before I sleep.
> The woods are lovely, dark and deep,
> But I . . .

Then it fell on its side and twitched and popped.

The Bishop handed it to Marcus.

'Take it to the Shih Tzu recovery room, quickly now.'

This had once been the office of a Reflective Replenisher who'd been carted off to a lunatic asylum.

All eyes were on the Bishop. The fly could smell the hormonal rush. The first power point slide said: LET THE SANDWICHES DO THE TALKING!

The businesswoman laughed with relief and the Bishop pointed at the nearest pile.

'They're not going to eat themselves!'

Twenty minutes later the Bishop continued. There were facts and figures and pie charts.

'We have academics who are on the old contracts and they're costing us money—holiday pay, weekend pay, and employer pension contributions. We'll soon be putting a stop to that.'

'Goodo,' said Roxana Grogan.

'I think we could cut fifty academics this coming year in what might be called a forensic cull. That sounds brutal, I know. There'll be lots of whining. The union will no doubt moan. It might get into the *Chronicle*. I'll take the editor out for a good lunch. We can demonstrate the positive side, namely a leaner and hungrier staff, more streamlined. I have spoken to the Minister for Education and she's enthusiastic. Friends, and polyamorous colleagues, we're at the cutting edge. We will offer plenty of counselling. It's important the academics see the bigger picture; it will make them feel better as they prepare to leave us. Of course, we can offer them work in our post-Brexit 'Eat Only English' supermarket sector. They won't have to do any grading when they're stacking shelves or picking strawberries and we can get them cheap housing in Shit Town. I've already had a word with the housing authorities.'

The audience was impressed.

The Bishop continued: 'In the short term I realise this letting go of teaching staff might create some problems when it comes to classroom delivery unless,' she now looked surprisingly impish, 'we get the students to teach themselves.'

'Good idea,' shouted Clueless.

The Bishop continued: 'Short term we will need to recruit more zero hour academics. It's getting a tad trickier to find staff now that it's become public knowledge we pay them less than the minimum wage. We might have to recruit directly from Shit Town. They will have to be deloused and fumigated before they set foot on the campus as well as vaccinated. The last thing we need is another pandemic, especially in the coming weeks.'

'Absolutely!' shouted Clueless. 'I don't want any Shit Town shitters in the library. Books are shitty enough without any of these people putting their shitty hands all over the shitty place.'

'Make suitable arrangements, Fred' the Bishop said. 'And exercise some compassion! We are, never forget, a values-driven institution.'

'Are we?' asked Roxana Grogan, swaying on her seat.

The Bishop brought a handkerchief to her mouth and coughed.

'All this, however, is small beer. Dear colleagues and friends let me cut to the chase. I want to give you a vision of the future.'

The next slide said: LET THE DOGS DO THE TALKING!

The Dean of Divinity was passing around a sheet so that people could sign their names.

'It hardly needs saying that anything you hear today is strictly confidential.'

'Thank you, Marcus,' the Bishop said and paused a moment. 'Ethelred, our university mascot, as most of you will know, was recently the victim of a vicious attack.' She paused. 'Let me say very clearly we are looking into that. We will find the perpetrators. There will be no hiding places. You will be aware the Home Secretary is canvassing for the restoration of capital punishment. I believe this reflects a public appetite for a more rigorous judicial system.'

Though even as she was saying this she felt an unpleasant twinge in her stomach.

'We do have some leads,' the Dean said.

'Thank you, Leech.'

'Nevertheless,' the Bishop continued, 'as we saw this morning Ethelred is not only on the mend he is coping pretty well with his Grade 2 IQ Shih Tzu Installation Programme. Dr Kim has been most helpful. Of course, there are bound to be a few teething problems.'

She clicked on a multi-coloured graph.

'Please note, the IQ grade Installation Programmes go up to Level Nine. There are, as you would imagine, higher costs for each installation but I think Grade 5 or Grade 6 will meet our pedagogical and assessment needs. I'm planning to purchase fifteen more Shih Tzus next semester.'

VC Nirvana was thinking of an Umbrian villa they'd come across last summer at a very reasonable price. It came with a gardener and a flock of goats.

'And this has been fully costed?' asked the Dean of Discipline.

'Yes,' the Bishop replied. 'Getting rid of fifty academics will create a financial surplus. The Shih Tzus will be able to work around the clock. No need to worry about annual leave—with water and toilet breaks of course—and they will be installed with appropriate academic disciplines such as Transferrable Skills, Employability Guidance and an ability to make inane pronouncements at the drop of a hat. Grade Five Installation will ensure the Shih Tzu is capable of grading student work; though we might have to go for Grade Six if we are to satisfy more rigorous external examiners. If we want the

Shih Tzus to supervise PhDs we might have to go for Grade Nine Installation. Let's cross that bridge when we come to it.'

She stood in a kind of trance.

'All depends on algorithmic functionality I believe. Shih Tzus will be ideal for University Open Days too. And student poop-zapping opportunities will increase exponentially. Think how much excrement will spread around the campus. We could arrange a poop zapping gala. The university shop will do a brisk trade in zappers too. Another money making university spin-off. We could have our own poop-zapping team. We could create a new university competition, something more interesting than University Challenge! We never do very well at that.'

'That's because the questions are too hard,' said the Head Librarian.

'Squid might have something to say?' Roxana chipped in.

'Let him say what he wants,' the Bishop replied.

'What about the Creative Writing Department?' the Vice-Chancellor called out, unable to resist.

'Gladys is a scientist of international standing,' the Bishop said. 'And there are plans afoot for an Entomology Department but that's a discussion for another day. I must, for the record, recommend the work that has come from our Creative Shite-ing team. Do forgive me, I meant our Creative Writing team.'

The governors guffawed. The Bishop was angry with herself. Angry with Gladys.

'What work might that be?' thought the Dean.

'Can I ask a question?' one of the governors had put his hand up.

'Please do Harry, or rather Sir Harry. Many congratulations by the way.'

'Will the teaching staff be exclusively Shih Tzu?'

'I thought someone might ask that. The Shih Tzu model has economic advantages and the dog has good personality traits.'

The Bishop put up another slide which showed a range of dogs.

'As you can see the Labrador, in any colour, comes in at around 100 K, and there are service charges too as well as IQ Installation costs. That doesn't rule them out in the future. This time round we could utilise the Shih Tzus in a cost-effective dog teaching trial with a special first time discount. We do have options however. For example I have looked at the Sausage Dog but at the moment the Installation Programme only has a German speaking model and I think you'll agree'—the Bishop put up another slide with audio-visuals— 'the teaching delivery is a tad Teutonic.'

The clip showed a Dachshund sitting in a classroom barking out commands. Even Roxana Grogan understood the meaning of schnell. Hearing the German language reminded Derek of the lederhosen he'd bought on university expenses.

'Nevertheless, if we reach a consensus, there would be no harm in trying out the Jack Russell, as well as the French Pug which speaks English with a French accent—unlike the sausage dog who doesn't speak English at all—and even perhaps the Pit Bull Terrier might do—if managed properly. All of which, once IQ programmes have been installed, are teaching-ready in a number of disciplines. They might join us at a second stage. And, for the sake of security, we could take on a couple of Rottweilers, at 150k a throw. They wouldn't have a teaching role as such but they could take the place of Campus Security, or at least beef it up. We don't want any saboteurs or animal rights activists, or un-cooperative academics, do we?'

The VC couldn't help wondering about the bowel functionality of a Rottweiler which had been wired up to a Shooter Pooter.

Chapter Sixteen

'O bird
You beat the air so strongly with your wings'

—*Joe Hill Makes His Way Into The Castle,*
Katy Evans-Bush

HE PERFORMING ARTS DEPARTMENT had made a punch ball modelled on the Dean's head. It was hidden in a storeroom away from any surveillance cameras, full of spiders and disintegrating copies of Berger's *Ways of Seeing*. Staff slunk into the room at the end of the day for a cathartic pounding session. When Harry got home that night his right hand was sore. There was a doomail from the Dean.

Dr Blink opened the doomail with dread. The atmosphere on campus had been tense. He hadn't seen Tristan or Humph for a while.

'Dr Blink,' the doomail began, 'I have not as yet received an update regarding your poem for the Vice-Chancellor's inauguration. As you know the ceremony will now be taking place at the beginning of September and I would like to see a draft ASAP. Can we meet Thursday next, nine o'clock my office. Please be aware of your borderline punctuality status —kind regards Professor Leech.

'PS Make sure you're wearing your lanyard with joy.'

The poem had slipped his mind. He had written a rough draft a while back. He would have to hammer something out. The evenings were getting longer. He took himself to the Pig and Whistle and drank a pint of Global Britain. He chatted with the fritter-fryers, the pawnbrokers, the pizza-makers and the Zimbabwean goat butchers. Norbert was on a bar stool holding a bag of pork scratchings.

'Cheers,' he said, raising a glass to his lips.

Harry found a table in the corner and wrote.

Back home he gathered his scraps of paper and looked at his Wob files and listened to Billie Holiday's 'Strange Fruit' on his time-restricted Blotify App (the cheap version). He dug out a half bottle of whiskey one of his mature students had slipped him at the end of a seminar. He covered the Wob's all-seeing eye with blue tack. At three in the morning he pushed the send button and went to lie down on his bed which needed only one more never-never payment. The Dean had wanted rhyme; that's what he got. This is how the poem began:

> The Crucible of Change
>
> Oh Gladys Nirvana, Euphoria Bliss
> you joined the academic community
>
> bringing a large suitcase of opportunity . . .
> You've fashioned a Crucible of Change
>
> breath-taking in its range . . .
> We've climbed the League Table
>
> because you showed us we were able!
> We are compliant and reliant.
>
> Reflectivity is the bullet.
> and with your help we've pulled through it!

We think Fiscal Rectitude better than moral turpitude.
You helped us develop the correct attitude:

wayward thoughts have been driven out,
(some of them have been mercilessly barbecued . . .)

Smoking, loafing and joking have been replaced by
daily sessions of dog-stroking.

Your interests in climatology and entomology
have nurtured the right doxology.

The university's engagement with spiritual doo-dah
has been as meaningful as the barracuda

deep deep in the ocean. Vice-Chancellor Nirvana
you are the magic potion, the forward motion

our peppermint, basil and cucumber foot lotion . . .
You are more wholesome than a Hebridean crustacean

You are a revelation!
Gladys Nirvana you're straighter and more honest

than a South American banana . . .

8.45 AM Thursday morning, Dr Blink was walking through the
Crimson Building. The train journey had been largely uneventful.
He'd had a brief chat with Trolley Man Philips. He'd ordered a bottle
of Simone de Beauvoir's Lightly Effervescent Water. Perhaps he was
unlucky last time. The bottle fizzed a little when he opened it and
he took a swig.

'Doesn't taste right,' Harry said to himself.

The open plan air-conditioned admin offices were already clicking into bureaucratic buggery, churning out spittle, the English
language filleted and made shallow by imperatives and meaningless communications. A couple of administrators were doing 'Stand-

ing Desk Days'—their bottoms upright and doleful. This would earn them wellbeing voucher points and an upgraded lanyard.

'Good morning Dr Blink', said the nice admin girl, the one who liked 'Not Waving but Drowning'. She wasn't as nice as she used to be. If you're going to walk down the corridor of the Crimson Building, walk in a more defeated way Dr Blink. 'Think of slavery as educational' Amiri Baraka had written.

'Good morning clerks', Harry said under his breath, his lanyard swinging.

At 8.55, he knocked on the Dean's door. For five minutes he stood waiting for the 'Come—I won't have you late Dr Blink, I won't have you early either.'

The metronome was in motion. The parrot had acquired a more colourful plumage—the ultra-deluxe model.

The Dean looked at Harry closely. 'Have you anything to say Dr Blink?'

'Regarding the poem?'

'We'll get to the poem in a moment.'

'I'm looking forward to Vice-Chancellor Nirvana's inauguration,' Harry said. 'I'm re-reading Lucretius.'

'I'm surprised you can find the time.'

'I want to read the poem in a meaningful way.'

'No one said anything about you reading the poem!'

'You're going to read it yourself?'

'Certainly not in its present shape. It doesn't seem quite "there". In any case I don't read poems out. I don't read poems out Dr Blink, and if I were to choose, I wouldn't fucking read poems at all.'

'Oh, the poem's not quite "there" Professor Leech!'

'I said we'd talk about the poem later.'

'The sun is shining,' Harry said, 'the sun is shining.'

'I think we could agree on that.' The Dean sounded bored.

'Isn't it lovely to agree?'

'I haven't arranged this meeting for an outbreak of facetiousness, Dr Blink.'

'I thought you'd arranged the meeting to discuss the poem.'

'That poem will be discussed in the fulness of time.'

The Dean stood up, walked around the room and sat down again.

'Do you have anything to say?'

He's digging. It was impossible to know how much the Dean knew or didn't know. It was difficult for Harry to know for sure what he knew himself. Perhaps the Dean had been in that helicopter with the VC? Did the Dean know about Dr Lomax and Stinker Rogers? Was the Bishop standing at the top of Trollop Towers right now, like Lady Macbeth?

'How do you rate Dr Black as a poet?'

'A poet in the Romantic tradition.'

'Is that why he lives in the Forest?'

'It's a beautiful place. I have walked under its shady canapés,' Harry said jauntily.

'Wiser not to have said that. You should seek permission before walking under shady canapes. For your own safety if nothing else. People are found hanging in the Forest, Dr Blink.'

The Dean took out his special pen and wrote in the sanction book.

Dr Blink had wanted to show his students the Brutalist Architecture of South Town. He had filled out fifteen pages of risk assessment. Would the Brutalism have a negative impact on students with mental health problems? Each time he sent back the forms there was another form. In the end he cancelled the trip. Which is just what the clerks wanted.

'Do you think he's a poet in the Revolutionary Romantic tradition?' the Dean continued.

'He's more Coleridge than Percy Bysshe,' Blink replied.

'Would you not say he was a bit Tyger Tyger burning bright in the middle of the night?'

'Not a tiger middle of the night bone in him really. More into Tits. Blue Tits.'

'From what little I've read of his work I would have thought Blake might have been an influence?'

'Would you?' Blink tried to sound non-committal. 'I think William Blake can be misunderstood.'

'I see. Misunderstood.'

There was a lull in the interrogation.

The Dean said: 'How would you get to the Forest from South Town? I believe you live in South Town.'

'There's a bus.'

'A bus!'

The Dean made a note: See if I can close down the bus service from South Town to the Forest.

The conversation gave way to metronomic clacking. 'Ten Minutes! Ten Minutes!' the parrot squawked. It had a Nigerian lilt.

The Dean looked at Dr Blink. Harry remained impassive yet his lanyard took on a guilty air. He wondered if he could hang on in there. He wondered whether the Dean knew what he was wondering. It would be sweet to see the Dean strafed by Nigerian parrot shit.

'When was the last time you saw Dr Black?'

Harry didn't like this line of questioning.

'Difficult to say. I sometimes catch a glimpse of him on the Bliss Train.'

'The Bliss Train,' repeated the Dean. 'Does that idiot Philips still sell Simone de Beauvoir's Lightly Effervescent Water?'

'I bought a bottle this morning.'

'Excellent,' said the Dean. He allowed himself a smile. The Lightly Effervescent Water was one of his business spin-offs.

'I have printed off two copies of your poem.'

He pronounced the word 'poem' as if he were picking up something from under his shoe. He handed a copy to Harry.

'The general enthusiasm of the piece is laudable enough I suppose. A little OTT in places. Let's just say it could be more nuanced. No? I'd like to consider several lines more closely. Concentrate, please.'

The Dean read from the piece of paper:

'You are the magic potion, the forward motion, our peppermint, basil / and cucumber foot lotion.'

Who knew that once a week the Dean made his way to the VC's office in the Fairly Old Building to discuss staff discipline? When the Dean walked into the room the Vice chancellor's legs were stretched across the desk. All he had to do was unlace the Berlusconi-Gucci boots and her feet were his for half an hour, or however long it took the Vice-Chancellor to come. University matters could be discussed later. Gladys had several bottles of foot lotion in her bottom drawer, bottles which had been bought by Terry and which made their way to the campus. She could play at home and she could play away. She was a Sister of Success. She undertook a daily regime of lip stretching exercises.

She'd created a pheromone spray from the Columbian queen ant. It was going to make her a lot of money. It would be called Nirvana. Boots had already shown an interest, not to mention several expensive boutiques in London. The Vice-Chancellor had got to know a Rear Admiral through her charity work and he thought the men in the Navy would love it. She sprayed herself liberally in the morning after taking a Bomba-Banga Brazilian foam bath. Terry had lost his handicap at the Trollop Country Club. He could hardly concentrate on anything. And the Dean was putty in her hands.

'Is there a reason you describe the Vice-Chancellor as our peppermint, basil and cucumber foot lotion?'

Harry couldn't have known that peppermint, basil and cucumber was one of the lotions in the VC's special drawer. True, he had seen Tristan's videos of those foot massaging sessions. Did the Dean's questioning suggest they knew something about the Blake Programme? Tristan and Suki didn't tell Harry everything. Just as well. The less people who knew the whole picture the better. Harry was happy to be a foot soldier, an academic dung beetle. As long as he wasn't going to be shafted. He didn't want to become a permanent resident of Shit Town.

The parrot was looking moody.

'No, well I mean yes, lotion rhymes with potion and motion and I thought it a nice conceit,'

'Did you now?' replied the Dean. 'A nice conceit.'

He looked at Harry.

'And why, if I may ask, of all the lotions there are in the world should it be peppermint cucumber and basil?'

Harry was thinking hard, trying to remember whether he had seen a peppermint cucumber and basil lotion in one of the clips that Tristan had shown him.

'In the old days,' he ventured, 'I bought a foot lotion with some basil in it. I don't think I could afford it now.'

'I should think not,' the Dean said.

The parrot squawked 'Ten Minutes! Ten Minutes!' for the second time.

'My advice,' said the Dean, 'would be to take that bit out altogether. Understood?'

'If you insist.'

The Dean was looking at the poem again. He read: 'You are more wholesome than a Hebridean crustacean / you are a revelation.'

Harry smiled.

'Smiling?' the Dean asked. 'Is this the moment for smiling?'

'We had a holiday in Scotland once. The borders were open then. We had this crab.'

'And?'

'The joy, Professor Leach. I don't believe I've ever had a tastier one.'

'And this makes you think of the Vice-Chancellor?'

Harry laughed. He hadn't laughed in a while. Much better than a dog stroking session. Laughing in the Dean's office was disallowed.

'I was thinking of the white meat and the clear blue water.'

'I see.'

Did Dr Blink have amorous yearnings too? The Vice-Chancellor's pheromone spray was very powerful.

'And then, of course, there's the rhyme. Crustacean rhymes with revelation.'

'Yes, yes, I know it rhymes,' the Dean said, rolling his eyes. 'But you could in equal measure go for "celebration". That also rhymes with revelation.'

'Yes, it does I suppose. A Hebridean celebration. Lots of whisky I imagine, some dancing too.'

'Dr Blink, I think you're being deliberately obtuse. At this juncture you needn't really have the Hebridean reference at all. It seems something of a distraction. The VC doesn't come from the Hebrides.'

'She comes from Shudderfield-on-Sea.'

'Yes, yes,' said the Dean.

'You are more wholesome than a Shudderfield-on-Sea celebration, you are a revelation. Doesn't quite have the same ring Professor Leech.'

'Oh for goodness sake, I don't mean changing the odd word. I mean re-writing the line. It's not that hard Dr Blink.'

'Back to the drawing board,' Harry said.

'Whilst we're about it, I think you could come up with something better than spiritual doo dah.'

'You told me to write that down.'

'I might have said "spiritual doo dah" on the spur of the moment but I thought you would have come up with something less stupid: spiritual values, spiritual development, anything really—not doo dah.'

'Doo dah rhymes with barracuda.'

'For fuck's sake,' shouted the Dean, 'anything fucking rhymes with anything if you want it to. It's just a question of moving the fucking words around. It's not quantum physics Dr Blink.'

'The right words in the right order.'

'Blink,' the Dean said, 'you're trying my patience.'

Harry could feel his lanyard relaxing. In fact his lanyard seemed almost happy now. A happy lanyard. It'd never happened before.

The Dean continued, 'Similarly, you may wish to reconsider the infantile nature of that line: "Nirvana you are straighter and more honest than a South American banana." What, in fact, is the meaning of "straighter" here? I almost have the feeling you are implying the opposite. Are you suggesting, ironically, that the Vice-Chancellor is crooked?'

'I abandoned irony long ago.'

'Good.'

Then the Dean said, 'I'm glad you're wearing your lanyard.'

'It hangs rather nicely, doesn't it?'

'Don't get clever with me.'

Harry, despite himself, stood up, looked the Dean in the eye and sang *'Is you is or is you ain't my baby. Maybe baby's found somebody new. Or is my baby still my baby true?'—'Is you is or is you ain't my baby. Maybe baby's found somebody new. Or is my baby still my baby true?'*

'Have you gone completely mad Dr Blink. Sit down at once.'

Harry sat down, a little flushed.

'I'll get you some water. I've got some Simone de Beauvoir's in the cupboard.'

'I'm alright thanks.'

The Dean sat down again.

'And, just between us,' he continued, 'I'm glad you didn't make too much of the churchy stuff. You might mention Ethelred to please the Bishop.'

'There's been a rumour he's out of sorts. Hasn't been seen for a while.'

The Dean looked at Harry sharply.

'As far as I know Ethelred is as fit as a butcher's dog. No need to worry about that. I'm surprised you've got the time to listen to rumours.'

'That's good to know,' Harry replied.

'Re-write the poem. Make the spotlight shine on VC Nirvana with a little light on me—if you catch my drift. I'm sure you could dig out some rousing epithet.'

The Dean's a money-counting machine, the Dean's a Turkish latrine. The Dean's a mockingbird jerking off to Jane Birkin and Serge Gainsbourg.

'I'll see what I can do.'

The African Grey having been returned to Lagos for upgrade had undergone a cross-species mutational lift with a Scarlet Macaw from South America. It rose from the table. It looked Harry in the eye.

'I am not Flaubert's Parrot. I am the Dean's Parrot. I am The Dream Parrot—I'm the Big Arsed Fela Kuti Parrot. The parrot which hears, which sees, which sheets . . .'

It pecked Harry's smoking arm and swivelled into the unleashing position. Harry threw himself under the Dean's desk. He could hear the splatter of watery shit smacking the chair. Sheltering under the desk, Harry could smell the polish on the Dean's brogues. The parrot squawked and let out another watery load. After a while the metronome stopped.

The Dean was impressed. The Dean was happy. He was almost as happy as when he emptied his bladder into those vats of Simone de Beauvoir's Lightly Effervescent Water.

Harry had been in the Dean's office for more than forty minutes. If he stayed any longer the parrot might scratch out his eyes.

'Our meeting has finished,' the Dean said. 'Unless you have a penchant for leather I suggest you get out of there Dr Blink. You have work to do. I'll have you know,' he said to Harry who was now standing up, checking he was free from any bird splatter, 'that the world doesn't revolve around fucking poems.'

As Dr Blink retreated from the office he saw there was blood on his arm and he could hear the Dean on the phone to Squid.

'Get your rubbery arse over here ASAP, there's shite everywhere.'

Chapter Seventeen

IMELDA WELLBELOVED slept badly before Revelations. She practiced meditation, mindfulness and some old-fashioned masturbation. It was this third activity which pushed her, albeit briefly, into sleep. Ethelred had joined in with the meditation and the mindfulness, assuming the position of his mistress, but looked askance when it came to activity number three. Since the removal of his testicles his evacuations had been ardently faecal. When he crapped on campus the Bishop offered up a prayer to Mother Nature and sometimes he was rewarded with a dog biscuit made of ginseng and vitamin D. He knew only too well that if he soiled the Bishop's bedroom he'd get another beating. How could he forget what happened on the day of the VC's inaugural lecture?

Ethelred had been programmed to read Blink's poem. The Bishop, after careful consideration, liked the idea even though it had come from Professor Leech. She realised it took some of the spotlight away from the VC and it would showcase her Great Pedagogical Canine Project. She had several Boom meetings with Dr Kim. A technician came down from London. She'd had some initial anxiety about the plan but she warmed to it after listening to Dr Kim's advice and she was impressed by the technician's enthusiasm. Ethelred was put through his paces. He learnt to read the poem quite beautifully. The Bishop couldn't wait to see the faces of the packed out auditorium. This might be Nirvana's inaugural event but the Bishop's Shih Tzu would steal the show. When the technician spoke about a musical entrée Imelda's insides fluttered.

'What did you have in mind Gary?'

'How about Puccini's "Nessun Dorma"? We could start rehearsals tomorrow. I'll need an assistant though.'

The following day Ethelred was plugged into a Shooter Poot and several hours later not only could he recite Blink's poem but he could give a commendable performance of 'Nessun Dorma', hitting the final notes of *Vincero, Vincero* with brio.

Imelda could see the headlines in the *Chronicle*—Move over Pavarotti. Welcome Ethelred the university Shih Tzu who is as ready as could be!

The Bishop spent several days in contemplation, kneeling in front of her triptych of aubergines and speaking to the Light of Idaho. In the future, the Bishop was saying, her pedagogical dogs would take on a proselytising role.

'That's beautiful,' said the American.

The auditorium was packed. Harry sat next to Tristan, near the back. Senior Management, VIPS and their friends took up the front rows. There were bouquets of flowers and Student Ambassadors were showing people to their seats. A mature student from the Music Department was plucking at the strings of a harp. Staff attendance was compulsory. Leech had sent a reminder to the teaching staff. No one wanted a Shit Town taster session at this stage of the academic year.

The night before the event Harry had received a doomail from the Dean. 'You'll be pleased to know your poem will be read by Ethelred—the university dog.

'PS. Please make sure you wear your lanyard with *jouissance.*'

The reception of the poem, Tristan was saying in the auditorium, might well decide the fate of the Creative Writing Department.

The Bishop's words of welcome were well received.

'Ladies and gentlemen, friends, colleagues, non-binary people, pansexual people, we're at the start of something quite momentous.'

The harpist plucked a little more.

Wellbeloved said: 'I hand you over to Ethelred, our most cherished mascot.'

The audience cooed.

Imelda could hardly bear the tension. Hints of Puccini flickered through the auditorium. The audience was agog. Saffron Fraud's mouth was open. The auditorium fly swooped.

The Shih Tzu started gyrating, as if he'd been watching clips of Elvis Presley on the Bishop's Wob Top.

Ethelred started shouting WHO LET THE DOGS OUT? WOOF! WOOF!—WHO LET THE DOGS OUT? WOOF! WOOF!

'Where's that fucking technician?' Imelda said to herself. Wellbeloved turned around and saw the audience was going nuts.

WHO LET THE DOGS OUT? WOOF! WOOF!

Colleagues from Performing Arts were joining in.

WHO LET THE DOGS OUT? WOOF! WOOOF!

Even the VC was on her feet, pulling Terry up alongside.

WHO LET THE DOGS OUT? WOOF! WOOF!

Squid was shouting: WHO LET THE DOGS OUT? SQUELCH! SQUELCH!

Derek Nobody was getting an erection.

When the music stopped people got to their feet and applauded. Imelda dabbed her forehead with a hanky and a small aubergine fell out of her trouser pocket. The audience hadn't expected 'Nessun Dorma'. The audience hadn't expected anything. Clearly something had gone wrong with the Shooter Poot but the audience was lapping it up.

Ethelred was saying 'I will now read Dr Blink's poem in honour of the VC who will be delivering her inaugural lecture on The Nascent Hexapod. The poem is called 'The Crucible of Change'.

Now the clapping was led by the VC herself.

Oh Gladys Nirvana, Nirvana, Nirvana,
Euphoria Bliss, Bliss, Bliss
you joined the academic community

bringing suitcases of opportunity, opportunity, opportunity—

breath-taking in its range, range, range . . .
We've climbed the League Table

because we were able, able, able, able . . .
We are compliant and we are reliant.

Reflectivity's the bullet.
We've pulled through it, through it, through it, though it.

We think Fiscal Rectitude better than moral turpitude.
You helped us develop the correct attitude, attitude.

Wayward thoughts have been driven out,
(some of them barbecued, barbecued, barbecued . . .)

Smoking, loafing and joking have been replaced by
daily sessions of compulsory dog-stroking.

Hooray! I say, Hooray!

Your interest in climatology and entomology
has nurtured a beautiful doxology, doxology . . .

Ethelred hadn't rapped like this in the rehearsals yet the audience were going for it. Wellbeloved noticed the dog was slowing
down and speeding up. She remembered Dr Kim's comment about
post-trauma personality disorder. Was this the beginning of a psy-
chotic dog episode?

The dog was tap dancing now, as if his assistant had tossed him
a silver-knobbed cane from the wings.

DO DA DO DA DADA DO DA DOO DA D A
SPIRITUAL DO DA, SPIRITUAL HOO HA
DO DA DO DA DADA DO DA DOO DA D A
SPIRITUAL DO DA, SPIRITUAL HOO HA

Ethelred stopped and twitched and pipped and popped. The
voice changed. He sounded like Noel Coward.

Mad dogs and English women under the midday sun.
The Vice-Chancellor's a lovely crab, the Vice-Chancellor's a
　　　lovely crab.
Oh Oh wouldn't you say? Wouldn't you say?

Mad dogs and English women under the midday sun.
The Vice-Chancellor is rather fond of the South American
　　　banana.
What a fabulous day! What a fabulous day!

The Vice-Chancellor smothers herself in peppermint lotions.
The Vice-Chancellor has beautifully regular bowel motions.
The Vice-Chancellor is very rich.
The Vice-Chancellor is a money-grabbing bitch.

The Bishop's shirt was damp with sweat and the aubergine in her breast pocket was turning into a Baba Ghanoush. The dog turned its back on the audience, put its head into a yoga position and fired out several balls of excrement like a Gatling gun.

The auditorium fell silent. The auditorium fly called for its mates. They were swooping down on the VIPS.

Someone shouted 'Stop sacking lecturers! Stop the proliferation of food banks! Stop giving more money to Vice-Chancellors and their wealthy friends! Get rid of right-wing bastards! Stop making England into a shit hole!'

Although it was strictly forbidden, several Study Buddies were taking pictures on their g-phones.

Tristan leaned across to Harry, 'I'd say that was the end of the Creative Writing Department.'

Ethelred recalled in his canine consciousness the gasps of horror and the looks of disbelief. Imelda had got up from her seat in the front row, dragged him unceremoniously behind the curtain and smacked him with such force he couldn't bleep for a week.

I love thee Ethelred, you are my favouritest Shih Tzu in the whole wide world.

The words had come out of Ethelred's mouth, true. He was, however, without blame. Even the Bishop realised soon enough someone had sabotaged the Shooter Poot. There were gains and losses. The Bishop had enjoyed a snatch of Schadenfreude when she heard the words about the VC. Nirvana needed pulling down a bit yet the Bishop's dog-teaching programme was potentially in tatters. They had planned to get rid of fifty academics on the back of it—pending some ineffectual challenge on the part of the union. The Bishop's plan looked a tad ambitious if her Shih Tzu couldn't read the right words of a stupid poem in the right order. Maybe they would have to fork out for Labradors after all.

Leech had flinched too. He'd suggested Ethelred read the poem, in part to curry favour with the Bishop, in part to make sure Blink wouldn't enjoy any kudos which might have come from his delivering the poem in person. Leech would have hated Blink to stand in the limelight, even for a moment, and in any case he couldn't trust him to read the poem in a serious way. Maybe he should have done. Yet the Dean saw, after *le catastrophe*, how this put Dr Blink in an extremely bad light. It was after all Blink's poem and he charged Ms Grogan with setting up a disciplinary proceeding with all the trimmings and she spent the next few days palpitating with excitement. If the disciplinary hearing went against him, Leech would take the opportunity to put in for a Shit Town Relocation Order with immediate effect. The perfect opportunity to get rid of Blink once and for all. The Dean could see a big bonus rolling into his account.

Wellbeloved said to VC Nirvana, 'I suspect it had something to do with the triumvirate.'

It couldn't have been Blink himself as the poem was his and he would have understood the consequences of sabotaging his own work. He would have feared potential disciplinary action and Shit Town Relocation Directives. When Blink asked Black whether this was his doing, Tristan said, 'Harry please, I would never have put you in that position.'

Everything pointed to Humph. If they wanted man-made language he would give them dog-made language. It must have been Humph. He was wearing rather expensive dark glasses. He said, 'Vous vous trompez! You don't understand. Non non, non.'

The VC had to make a rather awkward impromptu speech making light of the poem and pointing out the need for technological vigilance in this time of danger. In 2035 there was, Gladys reminded her audience, plenty of danger. She would have liked to have administered several karate blows to the perpetrator. She delivered her lecture on The Nascent Hexapod as well as she could. Her ego had been dented, a horrible sensation and an altogether new one.

Nevertheless it was received politely enough and although the event had been tainted it was not beyond repair. She'd taken the opportunity to lay out the university's ten-year strategic plan. She expressed her warmest thanks to everyone for a magnificent response to the challenges the university faced, confident there was a bright future ahead. Terry had got to his feet and clapped as if his life depended on it and his rumbunctious clapping forced the audience to its feet. The VC turned the pheromone dial under the podium to the max and the auditorium was bathed in hormonal love. She had been officially inaugurated as Vice-Chancellor Nirvana of the University of Bliss and also awarded the Chair of the not yet existing Department of Entomology. It was a department whose very existence depended on the success of the Weeping Aubergine.

The VC had never been in the loop about Revelations. The Bishop kept her cards close to her ample bosom. Rather like a twelve-year old child who's expected to believe in Father Xmas, Gladys still couldn't quite believe some impending aubergine transcendence. Yet if The Light of Idaho—oh she was tired of hearing about it—wanted to fill the university's coffers she'd believe in anything. She didn't even like aubergines very much but she bought a couple from the Co-op to throw into a ratatouille.

Late September the weather was serene, an Indian summer, a maharajah summer. Imelda had spent hours on the phone with The

Light of Idaho, fretting. Revelations would take place on the great lawn outside the library. Fred Clueless had ordered ten signed copies of *Studies in Hermeneutic Aubergines* authored by the Dean of Divinity—special gold-wrapped editions with aubergine-coloured spines.

'What a colossal waste of money,' the librarian said sotto voce.

Roxana Grogan walked so fast she left a vapour trail behind her. Saffron Fraud OBE had learnt she was on the list for another gong. Baroness Fraud in the House of Lords. 'Oh imagine that!' she said to her husband who was pottering around near the runner beans. Professor Peacock, Head of Play and Creativity, was making a Lego Theme Park which contained a Cosmic Walk with a mythological labyrinth. The Day of Revelations would also be World Labyrinth Day. She let out a long Lego sigh.

A synchronizing event in Idaho was planned. This was the first time The Light of Idaho had allowed the Weeping Eggplant to travel abroad—Deliverance Day in Europe. There would be more con-verts. In Vatican City the Pontiff scratched his head. He decided the Catholic Church would fight back with an outbreak of miracles and a more aggressive employment of holy relics. He instructed his cardinals to dig out the bones of saints and make an audit, not to mention the thousands of pieces of wood which were said to have come from the cross. The Pontiff forbade aubergines from appear-ing on Vatican menus, even though he was partial to an occasional *melanzane parmigiana*. He had to sneak across the Tiber and slip into a trattoria incognito when the urge became too strong.

September the thirtieth was the Day of Revelations. The new academic year was gearing up for hybrid learning. The students were back on campus, fully vaccinated. The Wob had been pumping out titbits for months. Only the Bishop, the Dean of Divinity and The Light of Idaho had any real understanding of what would happen when the Bishop opened the Tabernacle. The University of Bliss had become one of the most talked about universities in the country. Although Senior Management had made an effort to suppress the antics of Ethelred in the auditorium by closing down social media for several days their efforts had not been entirely effective. However rumours of a talking, singing, pooping dog seemed to be working in their favour.

Applications from foreign students were up. Student Ambassadors swarmed across the campus. Rival institutions looked on with curiosity. Annunziata Kumquat, the Home Secretary, had been invited to Revelations. It would be a welcome distraction from her campaign to reintroduce capital punishment.

Roxana Grogan, in a febrile state, pulled open drawers and wardrobes looking for an appropriate outfit. She threw her butt plugs across the room and into her untutored mind dropped the phrase 'a cacophony of canapés.'

She was thinking of the post-Revelations drinks party she was helping to arrange. At this late stage she'd come up with a beauty.

'Yes, a cacophony of canapés! That should be on the Wob Wob.'

She sent a doomail to the Dean.

Leech was in the panopticon office listening to his Newtonian balls. A non-believer, like the VC, he'd never been in the church's inner sanctum and was both excited and concerned. Excited Revelations would bring more money to his personal account, concerned that the Bishop's position as Pro-Vice-Chancellor would only be so in name as she tightened her hold like Agrippina. Her theocracy would be unbearable. Compulsory Zumba classes for all staff, management included, and that would only be the beginning. He had two horses to ride and he still had a lot of riding to do.

Grogan's doomail popped up. He groaned. 'A cacophony! Oh stupid woman, it's always a cacophony, I can't bear it. One cliché after another. Why not have a cornucopia of canapés, a Cabaret of canapés, a Neapolitan Camorra of canapés, a cruise ship of fucking canapés . . . ?'

The malodorous parrot flapped its wings and pushed out its tongue.

The Bishop bathed in coconut milk and tamarind and knelt in front of the Remi Mackintosh table on which a triptych of aubergines whispered gently, acolytes of the Weeping One. The weather forecasters were right. It was a beautiful September day with a faint breeze to sweeten the heat. Soon the hot weather was going to break. A storm was gathering mid-Atlantic. Every common or garden aubergine knew something was cooking.

Ethelred had taken up a prayerful position too. He imitated the murmuring sound which came from his mistress.

'Good boy,' Imelda said. 'Breakfast soon, now go and fetch your bowl.'

The Bishop had forgiven him for his antics in the auditorium and wanted to give him his favourite dish. A farm in Titchfield delivered the frozen hearts of slaughtered chickens. Ethelred whined with pleasure. Imelda grated an organic carrot on the top. She made Ethelred sit. She made him say: 'May I have my breakfast please?'

'Good dog, eat it up, slowly now.'

The eternal rattle of an empty bowl, the jarring rattle of dead men's bones.

Despite her Shih Tzu mindfulness classes with her Shih Tzu she could never get him to eat his chicken hearts in a civilised way. Chicken heart, oh chicken heart, she couldn't quite forget those moment in the Centre for Peace and Reconciliation and the procession through the graveyard under a full moon. Sometimes she pretended it hadn't happened at all and if she tried hard, and threw herself into her ministry, she could blank it out for days on end.

She had learnt from her mistake. They'd buried Larry Lomax safe and good but bones don't lie. How could she have imagined Stinker Rogers would find them? Dem bones. Dem bones. Dem dry bones. It was an augury, she realised. Stinker Rogers was destined to find them. He put himself forward as the sacrificial lamb. No chicken heart there. It was the heart of an archaeologist on the Camelot trail. She still believed King Arthur was somewhere out there. She was going to have a word with Eric Smallbone, Acting Head of Theology. He might get his trowel out and do a little digging himself. She wasn't going to make the same mistake with Dr Rogers. Once the heart had been extracted, his body dismembered—she later thanked her team for their un-dinting efforts, special gratitude payments on the way— the remains of Stinker were handed over to the notorious Shit Town Twins and they dropped them in a vat of acid.

It hadn't been cheap. Nothing was cheap. Oh Lachrymose One, let the money roll in. 'The best things in life are free. Another vacuous cliché which should be excised from the book of platitudes,' the Bishop said to herself.

Palimpsests and psychopomps. Divinity and Profanity. The Light of Idaho dropped a tear on the map of England and the tear had landed on the town of Trollop. As if Ahura Mazda (Light and Wisdom) fought Angra Mainyu (the Destructive Spirit); as if Maat (Justice) took on Isfet (Disorder). They buried the heart of Stinker Rogers in an unmarked plot in the graveyard to glorify the Light of Idaho. The American Light was Manichean, wasn't it? Perhaps the Bishop had read too many arcane texts. Perhaps she saw evil where evil had long ago loped off.

In *Revelations* John wrote 'They assembled at the place that in Hebrew is called Armageddon—where the Woman clothed in the Sun stood against the Whore of Babylon.'

Imelda was both excited and appalled by the idea she might have unwittingly become that woman. She would have rung her exacting mother if her exacting mother were still alive.

'I fear I have become the Whore of Babylon.'

'Something for the CV at last!'

She had shown the Light of Idaho she was zealous enough to transgress, a necessary transgression, and the Light was lending her the Weeping Eggplant which was surely a sign of approval. Obviously the Bishop had to conceal the way Larry Lomax had met his end—thousands of miles away from the Shwedagon Pagoda. She didn't like the idea of prison very much and all this talk about the death penalty gave her wind. If an opportunity arose she might have a word with Annunziata Kumquat. Exceptions could be made, couldn't they? Convenient the Chief Constable was a friend of hers. When he told her they'd found the bones of Lomax he knew he was delivering a bombshell even though he didn't know the half of it. Shame he told Rogers too. She told the Chief Constable the enquiry must end now. Another special payment on the way.

'A scandal could jeopardize our position in the League Table.'

'We are family Imelda. We look out for each other.'

It helped he was on the board of Governors. Lomax was a little shit. He should have kept his mouth shut from the beginning and Stinker Rogers should have been digging somewhere else. What kind of archaeologist was he?

The Bishop had imagined The Light of Idaho would understand. They had seen the procession through the graveyard and enjoyed the flare lights and the drumming. They said it was all so *ex novo*, charmingly original with a nod to tradition. They might not have known there was a human heart in the canvas bag. On one occasion, speaking on the Divinity Line, Imelda tried to work out what the Light of Idaho did know. She didn't want to spell it out. It reminded her of the confessional box. She could feel the priest's hot breath behind the screen.

'Pour out your heart,' said that mellifluous voice from Idaho.

Imelda found it difficult. She used the word 'sacrifice' and the Light of Idaho laughed.

'When I use the word sacrifice—my English rose—I use it as a figure of speech.'

That made the Bishop queasy. Later she stamped her foot and made the sign of the cross. The leg bone is connected to the knee bone and the knee bone is connected to the thigh bone and the thighbone is connected to the hipbone.

At three in the morning Imelda sat bolt upright 'Oh Ethelred, don't you hear it, don't you hear the word of the Lord!?'

The Bishop had never read *Crime and Punishment.* Not long after the evisceration of Stinker Rogers she swept into the library and took out a copy of Dostoevsky's novel. Fred Clueless waived the new library tariff.

'Happy reading.'

The novel pulled her apart and put her back together again. To transgress and atone, to murder and then be understood and even to be loved! Wellbeloved so wanted to be loved. The repentant suffering sinner taken out of the darkness and into the light. Imelda of Micheldever began wondering whether Julian of Norwich should have done a bit more sinning—perhaps she hadn't done quite enough—some wayward thoughts perhaps, a feeling of spiritual dryness, quite understandable holed up in a cell, some creeping doubts?

Dostoevsky's Epilogue was a prayer. Raskolnikov the condemned man—he'd murdered twice like the Bishop—was sent to Siberia. Sonya Semyonovna followed him and when the convict became ill he was put in the prison hospital.

He imagined the entire world *'was condemned to some terrible, unheard-of pestilence advancing on Europe from deepest Asia. Everyone was to die, apart from the few, very few, who'd been chosen.'*

The Russians understood brutality and salvation.

Would the Weeping Eggplant follow her to Siberia, or Wormwood Scrubs for that matter? 'Under his pillow lay the Gospels.' Raskolnikov had asked for the book and Sonya the prostitute had provided it, the same book from which she'd read to him the story of Lazarus. Imelda read the final paragraph of *Crime and Punishment* again:

> But here a new story begins: the story of a man's gradual renewal and gradual rebirth ,of his gradual crossing from one world to another, of his acquaintance with a new, a yet unknown reality. That could be a subject for another tale—our present one has ended.

It made sense. A pattern was emerging. The killings of Lomax and Rogers were part of a journey into sinfulness and righteousness. Revelations would be the beginning of a new unhindered, unfettered leap into purple glory. Ethelred's behaviour in the auditorium would become an obscure footnote. Her re-digitized pack of dogs would teach and preach and spread the word. She would be forgiven. She would be blessed. Dostoevsky's Russia was full of beautiful, evil, radical saints.

Imelda read *Crime and Punishment* several times. Her knowledge of foreign languages didn't extend to the language of Pushkin. She called upon Father Zhuchka her Russian Orthodox colleague—her own 'little Father'—and she instructed him to read in the original so she could listen to the music of the Russian language which made her think of the un-zipping and the zipping up of a leather bag. He would come to her office with its great Episcopal throne. Sometimes she would invite the Dean of Divinity too. Turning to the earmarked pages Father Zhuchka read from the Russian:

> He took the axe out fully, lifted it up high with both hands, barely feeling a thing, and almost effortlessly, almost mechanically, brought the butt down on her head. As if he were not even using his strength. But just as soon as he brought the axe down once, his strength was born.

CHAPTER EIGHTEEN

NORBERT HUMPED LESS these days, or at least the rhythm of his humping had changed. And Natasha nagged less. Sometimes she sang a folk song in the evening. Since that brief conversation about the poet Ana Blandiana Norbert was a lot friendlier. A few more Romanian names came Harry's way including Nichita Stănescu and Daniela Crăsnaru.

Norbert said, 'You must read Mihai Eminescu too, our great nineteenth-century poet!'

Although Harry had never talked about the university—conversations had mostly taken place through grunts and hand gestures, though on one occasion he had invited Norbert into his bedroom so he could show him the leg of the Romanian's bed breaking through the ceiling—it became clear that Norbert knew a lot about Harry. This was alarming. Was Norbert working for the university too? Which would explain why he was given permission to take the flat above a few weeks after Harry had moved in. There was no knowing. To trust one's neighbours in 2035 was naïve. And to make it worse Norbert had said, 'Glad you've met Magda.'

'Magda?'

'Magda Krol, a student of yours.'

'How do you know I know Magda?'

'She talked about you.'

Norbert offered him a Romanian cigarette, more subtle than Putin Plush, but with a distinctly fungal aftertaste.

'Don't worry, she says good things. She likes your class.'

'Something I suppose.'

They smoked on the wall outside the building. The evenings were lengthening. It was almost pleasant.

'I've read your poetry,' Norbert said.

'Where?'

The work of Dr Blink had been wiped off the Worldwide Wob years ago.

'There's a second-hand bookshop at the end of the Mutant Mile.'

'*The Street of Perfect Love?*'

'Yes.'

'How much did you pay for it?'

'Ninety-nine pence,' Norbert said, smiling.

'I think you were robbed.'

'I have it here.' Norbert reached into a rucksack he'd put on the pavement. 'Can you sign it?'

Harry patted himself looking for a pen even though he knew he didn't have one.

Norbert took a biro out of the rucksack.

Harry hadn't signed a book for over a decade.

'What shall I write?'

'To Natasha and Norbert,' he said. 'I read some of them to her and she got emotional. After that we make love. I write poems too,' he continued. 'I guess you didn't expect that. You think we Romanians are people-traffickers, drug dealers and bed breakers, no?' He laughed.

'No, no,' Harry replied. In any case his bed was cracked at the base and he hadn't been doing much humping.

A big hand went back into the rucksack and Norbert gave Harry a wad of hand-written poems.

'Read them later. You don't have to say you like them.'

'How do you know Magda,' Harry asked?

'It's not a short story. I tell you another time.'

The light was lingering. Natasha called out something in Romanian and Norbert went in. Harry looked at the reflection of the light on the windows of the hotel across the street. 'No Vacancies' had hung on its doors for years.

The fat owner with a South African accent waved. Little groups of nuns slid through his doors and then a few days later they slid out.

After the VC's inaugural lecture Senior Management regrouped. There would have to be some necessary damage limitation and a temporary pause button on the staff cull. The IT Department needed to check out the new cohort of Shih Tzus and make sure their delivery platforms weren't compromised. Perhaps the damage Ethelred had suffered in that attack in the Pro-Vice-Chancellor's office meant he would be forever vulnerable. Dr Kim flew over from Tibet with his assistant. Maybe Ethelred should be stood down. He could spend his retirement waddling around campus, left in peace to deposit illuminated packages which would gradually become less and less illuminated. He could be re-cycled.

Imelda shouted 'No, Ethelred shan't be re-cycled!'

The Dean was fighting hard to nail the triumvirate. To his irritation Humph ducked and twisted and it was difficult to land a punch. The Bishop seemed to be covering his back. And Dr Black had acquired some Foreign Office protection thanks to his American wife. Imelda wanted to minimise campus conflict until Revelations. Time to hold one's nerve. The union was demanding a meeting, a request which Senior Management wafted away as if dealing with an irksome bee. Gladys spent her mornings spraying pheromone at the ceiling of her office, waiting for her love-struck Dean. She wondered whether she should work on another edition of *Pure Reflectivity*.

The Bishop's energy was taken up in arranging the Weeping Aubergine's safe passage. The harmful effect of air cabin pressure meant the only safe way of getting the holy relic to England was by sea. The illustrious vegetable would be sealed in an airtight coffin and a fake death certificate would be issued. Home Secretary Kumquat had indicated that once in English waters the merchant ship would be given a naval escort. Imelda hinted the Home Secretary would be given an honoury doctorate for her troubles. Professor Lacan would ensure the Weeping Aubergine was transported quickly to the university once the ship had docked in Portsmouth. Imelda had enough on the pseudo-Frenchman to make sure he did her bidding. They could always give him the Stinker Rogers treatment later. The Light of Idaho was dealing with protocols at the American end. She had several Republicans in her pocket.

August the fifteenth, the university was having its annual two-week hygiene lock down. Teaching staff were barred from campus. Two weeks for the Dean and his security team to test facial recognition software and re-position surveillance cameras. Time to check offices and staff computers for any incriminating evidence of scholarly activity. Two weeks for Squid to super charge his Chattanooga-Hoover and get into deep cleaning mode. Roxana Grogan followed after him with a Germ Counter as happy as Princess Margaret with a gin and tonic.

The sun continued to shine. Harry had applied for a London Visiting Permit. The request had to be approved by the university and the South Town Municipal Council. He had managed to obtain two permits since the pandemic of 2025. He was allowed to stay in a Travel Lodge near Waterloo for a couple of nights. It gave him the chance to meet old friends and walk along the Thames. He saw that the House of Commons was covered with sheets of steel. Only its turrets were on display. The London Eye continued to turn. There were no tourists now. It was an enormous surveillance device looking in all directions across the city. He'd walked across Hungerford Bridge and gone to the National Portrait Gallery for old time's sake. The portraits were mostly politicians from the National Alliance Party, though there was one of King Charles in the Tower of London waving at a bunch of ravens. Buckingham Palace had been bought by a Chinese Tech company and the changing of the guard was made up of goose-stepping employees, erstwhile soldiers of the Chinese People's Liberation Army. There was a painting of VC Nirvana, refashioned as a Botticellian Venus emerging from her shell holding a copy of *Pure Reflectivity*. Imelda was peeved there wasn't one of her too. Post-Revelations that was certainly going to change. The 2025 pandemic lockdown hadn't been completely lifted. The cabinet held its Cobra meetings in Mortlake. Bollywoodian pictures of Annunziata Kumquat appeared on billboards across the city. Some were projected onto the Shard. Sometimes she was shown with a rope in her hand, smirking.

When Harry received an official communication saying his application had been unsuccessful on this occasion he wasn't surprised.

The following day Norbert invited him to a party. It was the first time he'd been in his neighbour's flat even though he'd heard his bed-thumping arias for more than a decade.

There was a large painting of a Transylvanian Forest as well as several photographs of wolves.

'I used to be a forest warden,' Norbert explained.

The flat was more spacious than Harry's and for an hour or so people clomped up the stairs. Norbert introduced him to a writer from Bulgaria. Natasha came round with cabbage rolls and polenta and there were little glasses of plum brandy. The gathering was noisy and there were impromptu toasts to freedom and Vlad the Impaler, which seemed to Harry an unusual combination. After several glasses of Țuică he was happy to toast anyone.

There before him, red cheeked and animated, stood Magda Krol. They talked about Czelaw Milosz and Zbigniev Herbert, though the conversation was difficult to follow because of the noise. Norbert took Harry by the arm and introduced him to his brother who'd come from Bucharest. Bucharest the Paris of the East. Hum Hum. Natasha and Norbert made occasional speeches, sometimes in Romanian, sometimes in English. Guests dropped into sofas. Pipes were passed. Dr Blink needed a little practice.

'Nothing better this side of Bucharest,' shouted Norbert, giving a thumbs up. Blink surrendered quickly, as if Shit Town had floated away into space and exploded into a zillion pieces.

Harry was loquacious. Norbert's brother worked at the Romanian Embassy. Norbert had gotten Five Day London Permits, he was saying. There were toasts to freedom and there were toasts to the Impaler and there were toasts to Norbert and Natasha. At some point there was even a toast to Harry. Even though Christmas was far away somebody sang The Carp's Final Lament.

'I'm doing a degree in Political Science at the University of Warsaw. I'm here for six weeks, maybe longer,' Magda said.

'Erasmus?'

'It's called Global Skilling now.'

'Fuck that.'

'You have to work round the system Dr Blink,' she said. 'Norbert got me over. He knew I was part of the Polish student underground and things were getting hot.'

'Out of the frying pan into the fire.'

'I do not have a frying pan.'

'I could lend you one,' Harry said.

Magda said, 'We must never forget. Our families lived through Nazism and Stalinism. Our families lived through the generals, Ceausescu, Stasi, Enver Hoxha, and Putin and all those corporate dictators. And see what's happening in the West. We're in touch with dissident groups here too. Dr Blink, I tell you because I think you might be one of us. We're fighting back. We call ourselves the Impalers.'

Bowls of potato soup were handed around in a fug of smoke. Daylight prodded its yellow fingers into the room. Harry was certain that over by the window he could see the one-eyed colonel raising a glass.

CHAPTER NINETEEN

'The world's greatest masturbator, who lives in Budapest, is masturbating...'

—*The Way Home*, Harry Mathews

SUKI WAS COOKING Tarka Dahl and grilling aubergines. Tristan was listening to Thelonious Monk. Suki had bought some monk fish from a passing van. They would have a good lunch today. Eating well is an act of resistance. The sun shone through the windows. If they'd had a dog it would be lying on the Bokhara rug. Suki walked into the bedroom and took off her clothes.

'Tristan!'

He walked into the bedroom, and they kissed. He hadn't shaved for days—post-Brexit blades were expensive—and because he had been smoking a joint he smelt like a bar of chocolate. She loved it when he quoted Blake—Tyger Tyger burning bright in the middle of the night. No matter it was the middle of the day. She opened his shirt and pulled him onto the bed.

A man with an eye patch was sat behind the wheel of a Morris Minor. He was making his way towards the Forest, avoiding the major roads. He drove slowly even though there was little traffic about. He was wearing a check shirt, a light blue cashmere jumper and brown leather gloves. He was playing with the radio dial and picking up surveillance reports. Some kids had been picked up for messing around on MOD property. He was enjoying the countryside and now he saw the sign to Brackenhurst. He opened the glove compartment to check the Beretta was in place. His leather gloves made a cracking sound, as if they were preparing to put themselves round someone's neck. He's been to the house before. He remembered it well even if it was off the beaten track; not that many tracks were beaten nowadays. The public was discouraged from going to the Forest unless they had an SI Note—permission to carry out self-immolation. If they were card carrying members of the National Party Alliance they could roam the Forest as much as they liked.

He liked the fact there weren't any neighbours, friendly or otherwise, to check on lifeless bodies, to find an old vinyl record going round and round and round. The Morris Minor was approaching Brackenhurst and the finger and thumb playing with the dial had found Elgar's Cello Concerto. Jasper barked. The one-eyed man put a hand into his pocket and took out a couple of dog biscuits. He tossed one over his shoulder and listened to the dog crunching on it, the other he slipped absentmindedly into his mouth.

Lunch was ready. Suki had roasted the monk fish and was letting it rest. Tristan was listening to Thelonious Monk. Suki gave herself five minutes to stand on her head in her favourite post-coital yoga position. Her feet pointed at the ceiling and she hadn't noticed the spider which was reeling down. There wasn't much space between Suki's small feet and the dangling arachnid. Tristan was flicking through Gramsci's *Prison Notebooks*.

The man parked the car five minutes' walk from the house. He let the dog take a leak and then put him on a lead. He took his jacket which was in the back. He put the pistol in the inside pocket and lit a cigarillo which he smoked with concentration.

'No barking,' he said.

An oyster catcher was flying over the trees. The man watched it pass and the dog sniffed.

The man, dog in tow, walked to the front door and rang the bell. Suki—still upside down—twitched and shouted 'Door!'

The spider reeled back to the ceiling. Tristan made his way to the front of the house. The man with the dog took off his right glove and the men shook hands.

'Pull up another chair.' Tristan shouted. 'Fetch another plate.'

Suki was standing now, listening.

'Impeccable timing,' Tristan said to the man with the eye patch.

The university was having AN OPEN DAY. The Dean spat out doomails for a week. Lanyards had to be polished. This includes you Dr Blink, the doomail had gone on to say. There was a dress code. Younger colleagues were expected to wear Bliss T-shirts. All staff were to catch the early Bliss Train from their nearest pick-up point.

The day before Harry got a doomail from SHIT BEDS ARE US. His direct debit had been uncollected thanks to a shortage of funds. Should this happen again, the doomail pointed out, the Bed Company were entitled to seize the bed. Harry imagined it would be recycled as 'a good as new' and sold on to another academic, bed bugs and all.

Humph was on the train as well as Tristan. The train was heaving and the air conditioning wasn't working. The automated yank voice was on a broken loop.

Have a Nice Day! Have a Nice Day! Have a Nice Day!

There were so many legs sticking into the aisles Trolley Man Philips struggled to push his trolley into the next carriage. The sticky heat meant there was a high demand for Simone de Beauvoir's Lightly Effervescent Water.

Humph was telling Harry and Tristan about a recent venture.

'I took the late train, the crepuscular train,' he said in a French accent. 'I alighted at Goring-by-Sea and in the fading light I painted an umlaut over the O so Goring-by-Sea became Göring-by-Sea. Instant Nazification!'

The Dean of Discipline stood outside the Fairly Old Building waiting for the teaching staff to emerge from the graveyard. Open Days! His responsibility. They were military operations. Try smiling, he snarled as the staff approached the campus. He needed to keep an eye on Lacan. At the last Open Day he switched the Muslim Students Are Us with the LGBTQ signs. This led to a furious letter from the local Iman.

Notwithstanding the pressures of the job, Leech was feeling pleased with himself. He had written the first draft of *The Definitive History of Masturbation*. The VC had signed off his Reflectivity Report.

'Oh Leechy!' Gladys had said to him in the corridor. 'This is clearly practice-led research and—*entre nous*—that reflectivity stuff is all bollocks.'

Squid had given the reception area a once over and Student Ambassadors were ready to welcome parents and their hormonal offspring. Electronic screens showed youths in a number of unlikely athletic positions, leaping, jumping and running through long grass in slow motion.

By ten o'clock the campus was throbbing. The VC had sprayed every part of herself with bee pheromone and a group of fathers was making its way towards her. If their kids didn't want to go to the University of Bliss they might sign up themselves.

Across the campus large flickering screens sent out messages of welcome:

89 PERCENT OF OUR STUDENTS QUALIFTY WITH A FIRST CLASS DEGREE.

IT'S OFFICIAL: WE PROVIDE THE BEST GENDER-NEUTRAL LAVATORIES IN THE HIGHER EDUCATIONAL SECTOR.

WE HAVE UP AND RUNNING TOILET TWINNING PROJECTS WITH THE UNIVERSITIES OF LAGOS, NAIROBI AND ACCRA.

WE HAVE WON THE GLIMMERINGLY SHINY UNIVERSITY AWARD MORE TIMES THAN ANY OTHER UNIVERSITY.

DOG STROKING, KUMQUAT MEDITATION AND ZUMBA CLASSES ARE AVAILABLE 24/7.

WE ARE A DOG-FRIENDLY UNIVERSITY—YOU COULD BE THE FIRST GENERATION OF STUDENTS TO BE TAUGHT BY A DOG!

WE ARE A HEDGEHOG-FRIENDLY UNIVERSITY. WE ASPIRE TO HAVING HEDGEHOG LECTURERS IN THE NEAR FUTURE.WATCH THIS SPACE!

CHINESE STUDENTS ARE MORE THAN WELCOME.

AT THE UNIVERSITY OF BLISS YOU COULD DO AN MA IN RESURRECTION STUDIES!

OUR STUDENTS ARE ENCOURAGED TO MOAN CONSTANTLY!

WE BELIEVE IN SPIRITUAL VALUES AND HAVE A MEANINGFUL RELATIONSHIP WITH THE LIGHT OF IDAHO—WATCH THIS SPACE!

THE UNIVERSITY IS ALL ABOUT YOU!

The Dean of Divinity was praying in the campus chapel. The Dean of Hilarity was hiding in the cathedral cloisters. Hardly anyone remembered him nowadays. Harry had some recollections of a white-bearded man. He'd guessed he was a visiting lecturer in the Theology Department. Bishop Wellbeloved had him removed because he refused to believe in God, never mind the Light of Idaho. Every time someone made a biblical reference he cracked up. The Bishop refused to induct him into the mysteries of the purple church, not that he wished to be inducted. The Church of England offered him sanctuary. He was made an honoury Deacon and offered a stipend on condition he didn't laugh in earshot of the Bishop of Canterbury on those occasions the head of the Anglican Church was visiting the cathedral. The Dean of Hilarity was chortling in the cloisters. He was having a chortling fit.

CHAPTER TWENTY

'Too Many Cooks Spoil the Dwarf'

—*Selected Declarations of Dependence*, Harry Mathews

'YOU'RE OFF to the Forest?' Norbert shouted from the window as Harry walked out onto the Mutant Mile. Harry pretended he hadn't heard him and walked on. It was September the thirtieth, and Harry was worried about Norbert's friendship. His poems weren't bad but how could he be sure they were Norbert's? And he didn't like the fact that Colonel Crunch had appeared at the party nor the fact he'd talked his head off for hours. What had happened to his usual discretion? He could hardly remember anything he said, just a trunk load of euphoria and Magda whispering things into his ear.

One night he'd woken from a complicated dream and heard a French voice in the flat above him. He needed to talk to Tristan and Suki and today would be the day, if it were not too late.

Teaching began the following week, if, that is, the Creative Writing Department hadn't been closed down. Harry had written a doomail to the VC apologising for the inaugural poem fiasco and taking the opportunity of sending the original and pointing out he would have rather liked to have read it himself.

She replied by saying the title of the poem—The Crucible of Change—was an inspiration. She added 'I will have to read the poem a few times to see if I like it. I have a feeling I probably won't.' She added a PS—'My advice Dr Blink is that if you are offered redundancy terms you take the fast-track option otherwise you risk being off the pay roll with a month's salary, maybe less. Your wellbeing is fairly important to us. I hope you and your loved ones, should you have any, enjoy a peaceful weekend. Don't forget that former university employees have bespoke shelf-stacking opportunities at one of our post-Brexit supermarkets.'

The bus to the Forest was empty and the driver looked straight ahead. A tattoo—BLISS—was on the left side of his neck. Revelations were programmed for six PM. It was going to be a fine September evening, the last throes of summer. Harry was going to the Forest for lunch and a day of waiting and a day of talking. Humph would be on campus—in his capacity as Leonora Carrington Professor. Harry would stay the night at Tristan's, sleeping in the Buddhist shed emblazoned with its slogan—'Choice Is Despair!' Tristan had pointed out they were going to have a good lunch with some damn good wine. There was, he messaged, something to celebrate. Harry would know soon enough. Tristan had got some mushrooms too.

The bus stopped at two villages on the way to Brackenhurst—Loaders and Droopington. No one got on and as Harry was the only passenger no one got off either. The bus waited at each stop for exactly ten minutes. Harry stepped out and smoked half a Putin Plush, keeping an eye on the driver in case the bus trundled off without him. The driver never spoke. Harry fiddled with his g-phone but no signal.

The bus stopped at Loaders and the door opened to glorious bird song. Then a peculiar scrambling noise and a Golden Labrador hopped on. The dog walked past Harry and made its way to the back of the bus. Harry turned and saw the dog was panting and looking out of the window. He wondered for a moment if the dog might start smoking a cigarette on the back seat. The driver switched on the engine and they set off for Droopington. Fifteen minutes later the bus stopped again, opened its doors, and the lone Labrador clambered off. Harry looked out as the bus moved off. The dog sat on the kerb, looking back at him.

Tristan in his Trilby was at the Brackhenhust stop, grinning. They hadn't seen each other since before the campus lock down in the middle of August. Harry had spoken to him from the red phone box a couple of times.

'Come,' said Tristan. 'Happy Revelations Day!'

'Is the university going to kick us out?'

'We'll have to see.'

They walked in silence across heathland, listening to birds, and watching rabbits.

'I saw the dog,' Harry said. He wondered whether he was going loopy.

'Which dog? A therapy dog? So many dogs nowadays. It's a dog world Harry.'

As they approached the house Harry began to tell Tristan about his journey but the trees began to shake and Suki was at the front door looking up. The silence had been broken by the throb of a helicopter and Harry's instinct was to run. The helicopter was hovering above the house. Everything in the garden had been flattened. The helicopter was above the field behind the house. It was going to land. A horse bolted. Judder, judder, judder. Out of the cockpit stepped Colonel Crunch in military fatigues. He was waving. Jasper belted out of the front door and threw itself at the one-eyed pilot.

'Down Jasper" ' the pilot said, rubbing the dog's head.

Tristan strode towards the pilot. The man took off his leather glove and shook hands. They turned towards Harry and Tristan said, 'This is Dr Blink, Harry Blink.'

The pilot said, 'At last we meet in person. I'm Captain Jack Bottomley.'

'I thought you were a colonel.'

'Never got that far,' Bottomley said, smiling. 'Kicked out. I got a dishonourable discharge I'm afraid.'

He took something out of his pocket, pointed it at the helicopter and a white marquee puffed up over the American chopper. 'No one needs to know I was flying a Killer Egg.'

They walked towards the front door and the captain and Suki hugged. The house was cool and at the back there was a walled garden with plenty of shade.

'Harry, you'll be wondering what's going on,' Tristan said.

Captain Bottomley took off his patch to reveal a perfectly good eye. 'They'll be looking for a one-eyed man so better get rid of the Captain Hook look. It did make me look somewhat louche.'

Tristan laughed.

Suki brought out a bottle of wine. The sun was up and there was a feeling of relaxation not unconnected with the aroma of the curry drifting into the garden.

The captain said, 'Harry, you were a bad boy just as we'd imagined.'

'Bad?' Harry said, alarmed.

'You talked for England at Norbert's party didn't you? I was impressed.'

'So you were there. I was going to tell Tristan about the party.'

'No need,' said Tristan, 'I arranged it.'

'You know Norbert?'

'We all know Norbert,' the captain said.

'The carp who's gotten too big for the pond,' Suki added.

'Writes poems,' Harry said.

'He does everything,' Bottomley said. 'Used to be in Romanian Special Ops, a pretty good drug dealer too. Perfect cover.'

'An Impaler,' Harry said.

'Humph's idea. Vlad the Impaler! He thought you'd enjoy that. Excellent people though. People we can trust.'

'And Natasha?'

'Writing her PhD on women of the revolution.'

'We wanted you to talk, Harry, to convince Norbert you weren't in the university's pocket.'

Tristan continued: 'You've read Orwell on the Spanish Civil War; you've read Hemingway. Different factions fighting Franco: Soviets, communists, anarchists, dreamers, poets . . . I wouldn't be able to run the Blake Programme without a bit of help from our friends. They need to be trusted, though, gold-plated. There's always the risk of treachery. You played your role Harry as messenger, poet, ears to the ground. Norbert needed to trust you. And Humph, notwithstanding everything, is a stickler.'

'I wanted to ask about him. I saw him in the graveyard photographs. I feared he'd crossed to the other side.'

'He had, temporarily, to get in with the Bishop. He didn't take part in any of the grisly stuff.'

Tristan rolled a joint and Harry looked at the dog which was panting quietly. He was still confused but the joint and the aroma of the curry and the silence of the forest were making him relax.

'Norbert needed to see the photographs too. That's why I left them under your door,' the captain said.

'Why didn't you give them to him directly?'

'We needed to show you were in the loop; that we trusted you with the photographs.'

'Anyway, he got them soon enough.'

'How did he do that?'

'He's got a key to your flat.'

Suki said, 'The point is we've carried it off.'

'Carried what off?'

Tristan explained. 'You know it's the Day of Revelations?'

'We all know that. The Bishop's been chuntering on about it for months.'

'Her big day,' Tristan continued, 'her apotheosis.'

'The Light of Idaho incarnate.'

'The light of my arse,' said Bottomley.

'At six PM this evening she will open the Tabernacle and reveal the Weeping Aubergine.'

'Eggplant,' Suki said knowingly.

'Whether one believes in the Church of the Aubergine or not, she believes in it, just as the Neapolitans believe in San Gennaro. Belief is everything. The unveiling will be more than symbolic. All the weirdos will want a piece of it. The university will leap up the League Table.'

'What do you know about the Light of Idaho?' Harry asked.

'It's a front for a right-wing Evangelical organization with a stake in the military industrial complex. Trump put a lot of money into it before he was sent to prison. It has its own scientists working on AI and it's branching out into space travel.'

Suki continued, 'The Bishop finds it hard to distinguish between belief and reality. I think she's crossed that bridge. The Weeping Eggplant will be primed, a combination of technology and magic—technology *is* magic. We've seen how it works in Idaho. There are tears, all the usual cultish hysteria and a desire to take out wallets and hand over wads of money. By all accounts The Weeping Eggplant shimmers and moans. Some people are repelled by it.

Many want to reach out and touch it. It must give out some kind of pheromone. One observer said there was something distinctly Eleusinian about it. It'll bring in bags of money, for sure. Well-beloved will become the university's CEO in reality if not in name. Nirvana will become redundant, I think. It's doubtful Imelda will agree to an Entomology Department when she takes over. *Pure Reflectivity* is beginning to get on people's nerves.'

'Not good for Leechy either.'

'Why?'

'He might pay lip service to the Bishop but the mare he wears his jodhpurs for is Gee Gee Nirvana.'

'I had a hunch,' said Harry.

The dog barked and conversation stopped for a while.

Bottomley took up the narrative: 'Sending the Weeping Aubergine to England was a wonderful opportunity. Thanks to the work of Tristan and Suki we discovered it was being sent over in a coffin on some Liberian freight ship, accompanied by a retired CIA agent. This is where Humph and Norbert come into it. The Bishop was sure Humph was in her pocket after the graveyard rituals. I think she's in awe of him. She sent him down to Portsmouth to meet the ship and ensure the hand over went smoothly. The Home Secretary had a word with the chief at border control. The ship arrived a week ago. By all accounts there was a storm during the crossing.'

'Captain B tackled the ex-CIA Agent and Humph carried out the switch.'

'Switch?'

'The Weeping Aubergine was sent to Norbert's. That's where it is now, above your flat Harry, safe as houses. Humph sent us a bog-standard aubergine via Box Fresh—it was the signal all had gone to plan.'

'I thought it'd been rather quiet upstairs.'

At some point during Revelations, once the Bishop realises she's got the wrong one, Humph's going to announce the Weeping Aubergine's in our hands. The Bishop ain't going to be happy and neither is the Light of Idaho. If they want their Weeping Aubergine back they're going to have to agree to our conditions. They can get rid of the dog teaching programme for starters. They'll have to bring back humans and they'll have to start paying them more than the minimum wage.'

'The Bishop's buggered,' the captain said. 'The university will fall to the bottom of the League Table. And I haven't mentioned Lomax and Rogers yet. There are nasty institutions in the grip of the National Alliance Party across England. The University of Pettifogging Bureaucracy, The University of Closed Minds, The University of Lies, The University of Pandering to the Market, the University of Moggers, Kumquat & Gove.'

'Lunch in thirty minutes: vegetable curry, pilau rice, homemade parathas, cucumber raita. Anyone want a cold beer?'

They helped themselves in the kitchen and they ate in the walled garden. There was much to talk about. It felt like a party. Suki told them about her encounter with the Shiz Tzu in the Bishop's office. One thing for sure, that dog can bite.

Bottomley said, 'I'm a meat eater by instinct but I have to say that's the best curry I've ever had. Any more?'

They relaxed in the September warmth. There was a pleasant breeze. Jasper was lying under the table, sleepy and hopeful. Bottomley was telling them about his dishonourable discharge.

A little later Tristan went into the kitchen to give Suki a hand. She was looking out of the window. He put an arm around her. Tears were rolling down her cheek.

'What's up Suki?'

'I'm feeling happy,' she said.

It was almost four now—a couple of hours before the unveiling.

'We'll go down to Bletchley Park in a while and see if we can catch the show,' Tristan said. 'I think we're going to have a nap first.'

'Some Egyptian PT,' the captain said.

Harry said, 'I'm going to lie on that bed in the Buddhist shed.'

'I'm going to stay here,' said the captain, 'and finish the wine.'

Harry looked at the Buddhist motto 'Choice is Despair!' and wondered if he had any choices. Tristan seemed sure things were going to change. Maybe he could get a travel warrant and visit his son in Uruguay. Maybe his citizen score would be pushed up and he could move into a rat-free house. Maybe he would start writing poetry again. Maybe they'd get rid of Leech. Maybe they would reduce his timetable from seventy hours a week to forty. He looked at the ceiling, took his glasses off and fell into a dreamless sleep.

Captain Jack Bottomley put his feet on a garden chair, stretched and dozed off. In his dream he was at the Court Martial being told about his dishonourable discharge. Tears were running down his face. By the end of the dream he was flying a helicopter over Libya, all pumped up.

At half five Tristan knocked on the shed door to see if Harry had woken up.

'How are you feeling? Suki's coming too. The captain's doing his own Egyptian PT. We'll let him catch up on his sleep. He can watch it later if I manage to record it.'

⋈

It was a while since Harry had been in Tristan's shed. It smelt grassy and stale. Tristan pushed open the small window.

'Leave the door open.'

Suki had brought Jasper on a lead. He was sniffing furiously.

The magus of broken technology cranked levers and dialled knobs. Suki stood outside with the dog, just in case.

They could see the great lawn outside the library with its ranks of invited guests. Student Ambassadors were showing people to their seats. Dr Philips was manning the cocktail bar—a free cocktail for each ticket holder. Tristan zoomed in and they could see Senior Management and their friends sitting in the front row: Gladys and Terry, Penelope Peacock, Saffron Fraud, Derek Nobody, the Deans, Home Secretary Kumquat, Moses Goodluck CEO of the Nigerian Parrot Company and there was Imelda Wellbeloved in her religious purple. Three rows back sat Humph Lacan, Leonora Carrington Professor, wearing academic robes.

Suki stepped in with the dog and took off her dark glasses.

'There's Roxana, I hope she's left her plug at home.'

Ethelred was lying down next to his mistress and Nirvana resisted the temptation to stamp on his tail with her Berlusconi-Gucci boot. She took out her pheromone spray and squirted her wrists instead. Leech had brought the parrot in a cage. The bird had learnt to screech 'There's only one Weeping Aubergine.'

There were scores of photographers and a choir of monks wearing Julian of Norwich T-shirts.

Imelda was breathing deeply and going through the words in her head. She looked at the congregation and she was sure she could see Lomax and Rogers. She looked again but people were taking their seats and she couldn't see anything. She put her hand under the seat and patted the Shih Tzu. Come on Imelda, get a grip. All you have to do is walk to the podium, open the golden tabernacle and the world will change.

Almost six o'clock. In the shed the computer began to pulsate and Norbert's jowly face appeared. Behind his shoulder was a picture of a wolf.

'Listen to me,' he was saying, 'listen to me. Magda came round with a Polish priest. He wanted to verify the vegetable. There's been a terrible mistake. Humph fucked up. He sent you the Weeping Aubergine. You've got it! You've got the holy relic!'

'Shit, shit, shit,' Suki moaned.

'Keep it safe,' Norbert shouted.

'We've eaten the Weeping Aubergine. It was in the curry.'

THE DAY OF REVELATIONS CONTINUED

A T FIVE MINUTES past six English time the Divinity Line gave forth its Gregorian chant. There was no one to answer because the unveiling on the lawn had already begun. The Light of Idaho left a message.

'Received a communication from a man called Captain Bottomley—Imelda, you need to get the relic back ASAP. The Light of Idaho is not pleased.'

The habitual mellifluousness had gone.

Imelda had turned off her phone in order to avoid interruptions but she felt a vibration in her pocket. My nerves aren't good. She looked down at Ethelred. The dog was looking glazed. All her praying hadn't brought any feeling of transcendence. That would come later, she thought. Surely. There were hundreds of faces staring at her across the lawn.

She needed to concentrate. She needed to remember the words. The monks had stopped singing. The singing, she felt, had been a little out of tune. Humph was getting to his feet. Stupid man. Sit down like the rest of them. Just because you won the Leonora Carrington Prize doesn't mean you can make up the rules. She had reminded Humph about the seriousness of Revelations. There are good jokes and there are bad jokes she said. Sometimes there were just too many jokes. When she looked again she could have sworn that Lomax and Rogers were sitting in the congregation. This was the second time she'd seen them.

'I'm going to be sick.'

She took a deep breath. She said a prayer and welcomed the congregation.

'I must start by thanking you for coming to Revelations. Nietzsche told us God was dead. I think Nietzsche should think again.'

Oh get on with it, thought Gladys to herself. Derek Nobody was getting hard. Wellbeloved faced the Tabernacle and blessed it and from her breast pocket she took out a golden key. Her hands were shaking. She could hear Ethelred whimpering. The Aubergine was wrapped in purple cloth. She turned round to hold up the glorious bundle to the congregation. Photographers clicked and clicked. People got out their handkerchiefs, some people got out their credit cards.

The Light of Idaho was watching from the Eggplant Bunker Room. Their fingers swept across the keyboard, pushing and prodding.

They were doing everything they could to shut down the broadcast. Nothing had ever gone wrong, and now this mess up in England! She'd rung Brock Mitchell Junior, Senator of Texas. He was their lead donor and he was planning to run at the next Presidential election. He'd contacted CIA agents in the south of England. Sleek cars were already on the way to Trollop Town. They were running checks on Captain Bottomley. He'd gone rogue years ago.

'I'll do what I can sweetheart,' Brock said.

They managed to close down the synchronised Idaho broadcast. Yet the unveiling was going live in England and across the Commonwealth. The Light of Idaho was beginning to sweat. This was a new experience and they didn't like it.

Imelda needed to concentrate. The words came to her, thankfully, and she spoke them. She could feel the weight of the goodly Aubergine under her fingers and she was taking off the purple cloth. The photographers had stopped clicking and she was aware of the silence. She could feel the warmth of the dying sun even though the breeze was quickening. An ominous cloud was eating up the fringes of the sun. She lowered her head and kissed the Aubergine.

The Q-phone in her pocket was vibrating again. Oh please stop! Her eyes were fixed on the great vegetable and that's when she saw the supermarket sticker. Humph stood up again. He had an on-person mic. His words were very clear, his accent was more French than usual.

'Imelda, I think you should turn the aubergine around.'

The Bishop wanted to tell him to shut up and fuck off but she did what he'd instructed her to do and she saw that on the other side there was a large sticker.

Humph said, 'Would you like to read the words to the congregation Bishop?'

Imelda was reading them to herself, squinting, as the print was small:

'Imelda, as you can see this is an aubergine from Tesco's—the Weeping Aubergine is in our safe keeping—if you want it back you're going to have to stop the dog-teaching programme and account for the disappearance of Lomax and Rogers. Game over—the Triumvirate.'

Ethelred began barking and Vice-Chancellor Nirvana was thinking 'What's going on?'

Two men in the congregation who looked uncannily like Lomax and Rogers stood up and waved.

'Here we are Bishop. We're over here!'

Although sweat was dampening her purple garments the Bishop decided this was a hoax. One of Humph's nasty little jokes. She would push on with the ceremony. Get a grip, she said to herself—speak the words and have done with it. She'd learnt them off by heart, almost.

'Great congregation of believers. Today I have the honour, thanks to the Light of Idaho, of showing to you this holy of holies, the Aubergine which weeps. Its presence here among us will change the University of Bliss forever. Our spiritual journey begins now.'

She lifted up the aubergine up and tried to kiss it again but she recoiled from the stench. No aubergine, weeping or otherwise, should smell like that.

'The stench of putrefaction,' shouted the man who looked like Larry Lomax.

The front rows of the congregation could feel their nostrils twitching.

The sun had been consumed by the black cloud and the breeze had stepped up a gear. It might have been the end of September but this felt like the onset of a summer storm. It began to rain. The golden tabernacle began to sway and when the Bishop raised the Aubergine up above her head in a great theatrical gesture it turned into a sticky pulp and then, as if it were a great porridge which had been over heated in a vat, it spat out in all directions.

A helicopter was hovering above the campus. Its throb was hidden by the thunder and the flashes of lightning which were getting nearer.

Humph was pointing at the Rogers and Lomax lookalikes.

'Some of you might remember the disappearance of these men. These are third year drama students dressed up. They're good aren't they? They might help to jog your memory. We say the Bishop had them murdered. We say the University of Bliss is a crime scene!'

The wind had blown the golden tabernacle off its table and people who had brought umbrellas were pulling them out of their bags. Not that umbrellas would keep their shape in this wind. It had turned very cold and a flurry of hail peppered the guests. Humph was shouting but no one was listening. People were scrambling to the carpark. Student Ambassadors were sneaking away, some of them were beginning to snivel. They wouldn't be receiving any gratitude payments. The Dean of Divinity was pushing through to the pop-up bookstore, trying to rescue his gold-leafed books. When he had a moment he'd have to write another chapter. This was hermeneutics gone mad. Roxana was thinking about those canapes going to waste.

The parrot was yelling 'Fuck Zumba classes! Fuck wellbeing! Fuck the Dean!'

The Dean had slipped away, leaving the parrot in its cage, his top of the range Nigerian parrot. Yet the wind tugged and pulled and fretted and suddenly the parrot was released into the storm. It saw a swarm of hysterical people who could be pecked and shat on but he had his eyes on the Dean. He didn't like the Dean.

Terry turned to Gladys.

'Let's get out of here. I parked the Jag outside your office.'

If the weather relented they could be home in twenty minutes. The following day weather forecasters would say Trollop Town had been hit by a meteorological anomaly. The wind was so strong the Bishop's robes were blown above her head. In her preparation for Revelations she'd forgotten to put on her underwear.

The lawn was becoming a churned-up mess. The congregation was running here and there as the thunder and lightning struck. Ethelred had done with barking. He lay on his back, paws in the air, rigid. Dead perhaps? Faint colours were pulsing from his ears. The Bishop looked at the useless Shih Tzu and kicked it with her Berlusconi-Gucci boot. And then she made her way to the bathroom to scrub off the foul-smelling eggplant which had stuck to her fingers. She didn't know that when she came out of the gender-neutral lavatories there would be two men in dark glasses with American accents waiting for her. They searched her office and disconnected the Divinity Line. They asked her about Bottomley.

'I've never heard of Bottomley.'

Three hours later she was on a flight to Idaho. She was wearing her purple robes. Although she'd scrubbed her hands several times they didn't smell good. They would never smell good.

⤫

Terry drove in silence. He put the heating on.

The Vice-Chancellor said, 'Did you notice anything strange when Imelda's cloak flew above her head?

'She wasn't wearing any pants.'

'I saw something hanging between her legs.'

'A *membrum virile*?' he asked.

⤫

Roxana had managed to extricate herself from the throng and she was walking quickly to her office. Someone had tampered with the signage—THE OFFICE OF CONTINUOUS PRIAPIC MOVEMENTS. When she opened the door she saw that her latest purchase had climbed out of the drawer and was dragging itself across the room. As she looked at it it seemed to be getting larger. It was pulling itself along with intent and it was pulling itself towards her.

'I don't really like it here anymore.'

Perhaps it was time to get another job. She deserved a more generous salary. There must be other universities which needed deep cleaning and reams of meaningless bureaucracy.

The Dean was soaked when he got to the car. It was misting up and he lowered the window to let in some air. Difficult to pin down the flurry of competing thoughts. I suppose that's the end of the Bishop and all that spiritual shite, argued one part of his mind. About time. He could now concentrate on screwing the staff. No therapy dogs coming to their rescue either. But what would the Revelations debacle do in terms of reputational damage? The university was probably sliding down the League Table even as he turned on the windscreen wipers.

The parrot could see the Dean was winding up the window. The window of opportunity was closing. The parrot accelerated and its beak crashed through the closing gap and plunged into the Dean's right arm. The pain was indescribable.

'Fucking, fucking, fucking parrot!' the Dean yelled.

The parrot's head was one side of the window, the rest of its body on the other. It was trapped. The Dean managed to slide across to the passenger seat and he opened the door with difficulty. He knew there was a pole in the boot. He carried the pole in his left hand but he had enough anger to smash the parrot to pieces. He wielded it with such force he cracked the window.

'You're not the Dean's parrot, mate. In fact, you're no longer fucking anything.'

When he opened the car door there were feathers everywhere.

'If I come across Moses fucking Goodluck I'll give him a beating too.'

He could hardly hold the steering wheel as he slid away from the campus.

The rain continued to fall as he drove slowly towards the suburbs. He was aware blood was running down his arm. Up ahead he could see a roadblock. He guessed the police were redirecting traffic because of local flooding. When he got nearer he could see several men in balaclavas. One of them came up and tapped on his window. The man took off the mask. It was Dr Philips.

'Fucking Inappropriate Philips, what the fuck do you think you're doing? Let me through you fucking idiot!'

'You see those men over there, next to that van,' Philips said, 'they are going to drive you to Shit Town. We've booked you in for a long-term residency. You can have this loo roll if you like, to get you started. And here's a bottle of Simone De Beauvoir's Lightly Effervescent Water. It's on the house.'

A couple of miles away Terry's Jag was making its way rather slowly towards their eight-bedroomed house. Gladys was saying 'Can't you go a bit faster?'

When Terry looked at his wife he saw that her glasses were steaming up. He put his hand on her leg.

'At least you won't have to worry about Imelda anymore. I'm sure you can double your salary now that sanctimonious bitch is out of the way. You'll just have to cut the lecturers' pay even more. It'll be a relief not having talk about the Light of Idaho. I never bought it myself.'

Terry was surprised to see a university van blocking the road. 'Look over there,' he said to Gladys, 'isn't that the funny cleaning man?'

Squid was approaching the car, holding a large umbrella.

'See what he wants,' Gladys said.

'Great Vice-Chancellor and honourable husband of the Great Vice-Chancellor—such horrible weather. Such a discombobulating day! I would like you to get out of your car—such a lovely car, such a very clean car—and come along with me. I will hold the umbrella like so. You needn't worry about getting wet.'

'What are you talking about?'

'I've been instructed to take you to your new lodgings.'

Gladys was thinking of opening her door and making a run for it but there was a man in a balaclava standing on the pavement.

'Our "lodgings" are down there,' Terry said.

'There are going to be some changes I'm afraid,' Squid continued. 'The University of Bliss has dropped to the bottom of the League Table and the Governors have decided they want to redeploy your services, Vice-Chancellor. You're costing them a great deal of money.'

Terry and Gladys were now in the university van. The man in the balaclava was sitting next to them. Gladys was saying 'I deserve every penny I get.' She was looking for her pheromone spray but she'd left it in the Jag.

Squid continued, 'You can take this Vice-Chancellor.'

He gave Nirvana a notebook: *My Reflections on Shit Town* written on the cover.

'We heard you wanted to write another bestseller. You've got six months to finish it. I'm sure you'll make an excellent job of it. You ought to know the Dean will be living at the end of your street, one of the shittiest streets in Shit Town, so no reason why your foot massages can't continue. Mind you they'll probably be a whole lot shittier than the ones he used to give you, if you catch my drift. We'd better get going driver.'

Gladys looked at Terry, 'Do something you useless fool.'

Julian Stannard has published nine collections of poetry, his latest being *Please Don't Bomb the Ghost of My Brother* (Salt, UK, 2023). He is a Reader in English and Creative Writing at the University of Winchester (UK). He used to teach at the University of Genoa, and *Sottoripa: Genoese Poems*—a bilingual publication—was published by Canneto in 2018. He has been the recipient of Bogliasco and Hawthornden Fellowships and his work has been nominated for Forward and Pushcart Prizes. He has received the International Troubadour Prize for Poetry and in 2024 he was awarded the Lerici Anglo-Liguria Prize for his contribution to Italian letters. Short fiction has appeared in *Exacting Clam*. His *New and Selected Poems* is published by Salt.

His website is www.julianstannardauthor.com.